Reviews of
No Gray Twilights

"Big Bay is a very special place full of genuine heartwarming characters that reinforce the resilience of friendship, loyalty and love in the face of adversity, darkness and deceit. I relish Richard Alan Hall's unique gift to succinctly write such emotionally rich and vivid scenarios that keep every chapter exquisitely consumable, profoundly fueling the readers own courage to face whatever may come in their own life. **No Gray Twilights** continues Richard's Big Bay tour-de-force series for so masterfully delivering very touching and powerful lessons of love and triumph of the human spirit - adventures no heart wants to miss."

— Brenda DeNoyer Girolamo,
Artist and Author, Derry, New Hampshire

"Richard Alan Hall is a marvelous story teller who can draw you all the way in by your heart and soul. His tales will make you laugh (yes, out loud) and, within a chapter or two, there will be tears rolling to your cheeks as your heart swells with the very joy of life. **No Gray Twilights** is a novel about friendship, love, and bonds that defy the realities of life, with dedication, and epic heroism by everyday people. Most of all, within the storylines, Richard presents each of us with ideas and models for how to live extraordinary lives with caring and kindness while doing the most ordinary of things. What a masterpiece."

— Pat Mazor, Author, Amarillo, Texas

"Richard Alan Hall has such a depth of compassion in his writing that the reader feels as if they are in the story with the characters. This is remarkable work. Seldom will we find a novel so clearly stating love and compassion for the human race. The ending will leave you wanting more."

— Donna M. Eriksen, Charlottenberg, Sweden

"Mr. Richard Alan Hall has done it again. He has touched our lives with his unforgettable characters in **No Gray Twilights**. His characters teach us to love and care for each other unconditionally even in the most difficult times. As he brings new members into the fold, we continue to learn more about "The Usual Suspects". They are as interesting and humorous as ever. The tale is woven in such a way that what seems at first unbelievable makes perfect sense in the end. If you have ever been to Key West you can just see in your mind's eye the events that unfold. It was an honor to have the opportunity to review Richard's third book and I am looking forward to the fourth in the series. You won't be able to get enough of his family of characters from Big Bay and beyond."

— Jane Stauffer, Between the Covers Book Club,
Elk Rapids, Michigan

"With only one eye, the character Richard Elmore Fortin's vision is prophetic, determined and right on. Richard Alan Hall has included us, the reader, in the close-knit circle of friends who lead us through **No Gray Twilights**. The violence is a good violence, resulting in justice for those the author has enticed us to care for, and even embrace. The love is pure and strong. The spiritually is straight from the soul of some very unique characters. This novel, the third in this series, is entertaining and over the top!"

— Adell Maksimowicz, Wedding Officiant,
Traverse City, Michigan

"I absolutely loved **No Gray Twilights**. My favorite of his three novels so far! I smiled reading Wendell's words, "They didn't want anything to with her...kicked her ass out, with her baby, kicked them out...what the hell!" The guys at Poor Joe's remind me of many of my tough, loyal and incredibly big-hearted friends from the street. Really loved every moment reading this one!"

— Julie Greene, Missionary to Haiti and India

Don't miss the start of the adventures with the "usual suspects"
in the **Big Bay Series** novels by —

Richard Alan Hall

Remarkable

Seldom As They Seem

No Gray Twilights

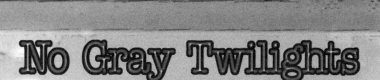

No Gray Twilights

a **Big Bay** Novel

Richard Alan Hall

Dare mighty Things !

Richard Alan Hall

rahBOOKs
keep it under your hat publisher

Printed in the United States of America

Book design and layout by Janet Mortensen-Chown

To contact the author, email: rahall49684@gmail.com

Visit the author's Facebook page at: Richard Alan Hall-Author

To order additional copies, call
Big Bay world headquarters @ 800-587-2147

rahBOOKs
keep it under your hat publisher

"Far better is it to dare mighty things, to win glorious triumphs, even though checkered by failure, than to rank with those poor spirits who neither enjoy much nor suffer much, because they live in that gray twilight that knows neither victory nor defeat"

— *Theodore Roosevelt*

To Debra Jean Hall. She inspires me every day.

Acknowledgements

Thank you to Debra Jean Hall and artist Janet Mortensen-Chown for creating **No Gray Twilights**' cover.

Thank you to my editor, Lisa Mottola Hudon. She did the hard work, again.

Thank you to Jill Beauchamp for her invaluable assistance. She made this a better book.

Thank you to Mary Smith.

Thank you to my wife, Debra Jean Hall. This is her fault.

And thanks always to our Eternal Daddy.

Table of Contents

No Gray Twilights

Prologue

It is not during our glorious days, the times we are surrounded by the smiling faces, that we are aware, but rather it is during the days when we feel blue, when our plans have unraveled, the times when the dream has vanished into disappointments; it is during the gray times in our lives when we realize the special ones did not leave when the smiling faces departed, and these loving ones are vanquishing the darkness in our lives with a wink and a smile and a whispered, "I love you." They are the rare ones, and they are precious.

— Richard Alan Hall

Chapter One

A Precious Baby Boy

Sarah Phillips pushed the doorbell button while holding her baby who was crying incessantly, his face red. She shifted her newborn to the other arm and pushed the doorbell twice more.

Stanley flipped the porch light switch on and opened the front door.

"Help me…please," the young Mennonite girl said between sobs, looking up.

"Please help me."

His mind flashed back…crawling on the wet pavement into the demolished vehicle; ignoring the prickling glass slivers in his palms and shards piercing through his dress pants, slicing the flesh on both knees; fuel pouring from a ruptured yellow dump truck; perching precariously on her crushed, upside down blue Pontiac and looking up at her blond braids dangling down from the suspended face, blood dripping from the tip of her nose, splashing on his face, the iron taste when it dripped in his mouth. Then a hot concussive push against his back as the fuel exploded…

…can't breathe…

"Hi, Sarah," Stanley said. He turned towards the living room and shouted, "Danielle!"

Sarah's blond complexion looked translucent.

*...bet her hemoglobin is eight or nine...*Stanley thought as they walked towards Danielle. He held the new mother's quivering hand, feeling the cold.

"I had a boy," she announced, extending the screaming baby towards Danielle.

Danielle held the child, squeezing him against her breasts and whispering, looking into his eyes, rocking back and forth. The room became silent.

"I don't have a name for him, and I can't keep him."

"When did you have him?" Danielle asked, sitting on the couch, side by side with the trembling teenager.

"Two days ago. My parents say I've gotta give him up for adoption," the high school senior sobbed. "My father says he's not welcome in our house. He said my baby's the product of sin and is not welcome."

Stanley shivered and clenched his jaw.

Danielle pulled Sarah closer and with their foreheads touching, whispered, "He is a precious baby boy and Jesus loves him every bit as much as he loves each of us, Sarah. Your parents are wrong. Stan and I will help...and you can stay here in the spare bedroom until we get things sorted out."

She shot Stanley the look.

Stanley leaned back in his easy chair, stretching for the telephone.

"Hi, Kate, Stan here. Need for you and Doug to come over."

"OK," Pastor Katherine Kennedy McGinnis answered. "Are you guys all right?"

"Tell Doug to get dressed; we have a baby to name."

And then Stanley called his friend, Judge Faith Linsenmayer, at her vacation cottage on the west shore of Big Bay. He grinned when she answered.

Chapter Two

A True Believer

The man opened the screen door with the *Closed* sign wedged behind the wooden spindles and walked into Poor Joe's Bar.

Timothy looked up from behind the counter. Dora looked over from the kitchen area and sprinkled chopped onions on the Swiss steak.

"We open at 11 on Tuesdays," Timothy said, studying the man's face, which had a large scar extending from the right cheek, up his broad forehead, ending in a cowlick at the hairline.

"Saw the sign," the man retorted. He walked towards the counter. Timothy put the inventory sheet on the bar and felt for his revolver under the counter with his left hand.

"How can we help?" Timothy asked. Dora inched closer to the telephone in the kitchen.

"Hoping for a cup of coffee; been a long trip," the man replied.

"Just finished making a fresh pot," Dora blurted. "Cream and sugar?"

"Black with Dr. Daniels, if you don't mind," he replied with a crooked smile.

The man's right eye was glass in a socket that did not blink, just staring straight ahead.

"What brings you to Big Bay?" Timothy asked.

The man pulled out a bar stool in front of Timothy and placed a brown suitcase on the floor. He sat down.

"A Pontiac, I think."

"Not what…why?"

The man laughed, his right eye staring without emotion. "Just having fun with you, Timothy. Damned if I know"

"You have me at a disadvantage, mister…know my name. What's yours?"

"Richard Elmore Fortin, originally from Estherville, Iowa by way of the big wild world, thanks to various adventures."

He sipped the cup of doctored black coffee and then nodded towards Dora. "Very good!"

"It's been quite a rodeo, by the looks of your face," Timothy said, watching intently.

Richard laughed with a crooked smile. "You should see the other guys. Oh, guess you can't cuz they're no longer inhabitants on Mother Earth." And he stared back at Timothy, his glass eye not blinking.

"So how'd you come to know my name, stranger?"

"We've a common acquaintance," Richard replied. "…Told me all about you and Big Bay…really thinks highly of you, says you're a decorated veteran, you and some of the guys livin' here at the bar…not to be messed with, that you're all trusting and true."

"Mind sharing?"

"Captain Quinn O'Malley."

Timothy turned towards the Goebel Beer mirror, reaching for his coffee mug, studying Richard's reflection in the glass. He turned back after a sip.

"How do you know Quinn O'Malley?"

"Worked with him for a number of years."

"Fisherman, huh?"

'Nope, flew helicopters."

Timothy put the mug down, leaning closer to Richard.

"When?"

"A while back. Lost my eye to an adventure in Honduras and there went my depth perception. So here I am, unemployed. Quinn thought perhaps you'd know of work."

Timothy's back and neck muscles relaxed and he grinned. "He did, huh? So you flew with the True Believers?"

"Yes, sir, I am honored to say I have."

"One more question. You in on the rescue of my wife in Mexico City?"

"Yes, sir!" He blew on his hot coffee. "She was flown to El Paso in my machine. I hugged her and your son when we landed. Damn, that was a close one."

Timothy walked around the end of the bar, sat next to Richard, and shook his hand.

"Thanks, Richard. I owe you, man. What's in the case?" he said, pointing at the brown case on the floor.

"Tools of the trade," Richard replied. He lifted the case, placed it on the counter, and released the two fasteners.

Timothy looked into the open case displaying three handguns and a dismantled sniper rifle.

Richard shrugged. "Only need one good eye with that one," he said.

Timothy leaned back against the bar. "Quinn was correct. I have a job for you. Lost my bouncer to the Methodist preacher."

Richard smiled. He closed the case, snapping the fasteners.

"Your room is at the top of the stairs, first door to the right. I'll introduce you to the guys over lunch." He paused. "Carla's going to love having you in town, Richard."

Richard went up the stairs.

Timothy walked to the pay telephone booth in the hallway next to the restrooms and closed the door. He dialed a number memorized long ago.

"O'Malley's Charter Service."

"Just met one of your first mates, Quinn."

"Thought you'd be calling, Timothy. Richard is one hell of a man, fearless. Since Doug's been domesticated, figured you could put his skills to work up there."

"Thanks, Quinn."

The connection clicked silent.

Chapter Three

Septic Shock

"**I** took Sarah and her baby to the walk-in clinic this morning," Danielle said, looking at Stanley's reflection in the mirror, brushing her hair while he undressed for bed.

"Why?"

"She felt warm and I was right. Had a temp of 101. They started amoxicillin and want to see her again tomorrow."

"Any idea what's causing the temp?"

"They drew some blood, should have the results when we go back…nothing obvious during the exam."

"They draw a blood culture?"

"Nope. They drew a CBC and electrolytes."

"She kinda looks septic to me, her pale flushed cheeks. Wish they'd drawn a blood culture," Stanley said. He climbed into bed and adjusted the pillow.

"I'll insist if her white count is up," Danielle replied as she joined her husband in bed, the man she had met when she moved from New Orleans, a new nurse in the Big Bay General Cardiac Care Unit, and he was the Cardiac Care Unit Manager.

"Wish they'd drawn one before they started antibiotics."

They cuddled and fell asleep.

CRASH…TINKLE…THUD

A loud crashing vibration interrupted the silent darkness, followed by glass tinkling on the hardwood floor, a soft thump, and the shrill screaming of a baby.

"MOMMY…mommy…mommy…" from further down the hall, from four year old Chloe. "MOMMY!"

Stanley and Danielle sat up in the darkness and threw off the sheet. Danielle switched on the bedside lamp. For an instant they stared at each other, trying to comprehend the interruption.

They leapt out of bed, naked. Both grabbed their bathrobes from the chair next to the bed and ran down the hallway towards the crying.

Danielle ran into Chloe Norma's room and lay down beside their frightened daughter.

Stanley walked into the guest room, tying his bathrobe belt. Sarah lay flat on her back, surrounded by little pieces of glass from a shattered full-length wall mirror. Blood oozed through her nightgown, flowing in little streams through the shattered glass. Her eyes looked at the ceiling without recognition, blinking slowly. Stanley knelt in the glass and blood and felt a weak, thready, rapid carotid pulse. She breathed with shallow respirations.

"Danielle…need help in here!" he shouted towards the door. "Don't bring Chloe!"

Together they repositioned Sarah with her legs elevated on a footstool. Danielle covered her with a quilt.

"Post-partum hemorrhage," Danielle said. She reached for the telephone.

"I think she's septic, too," Stanley said. "Damn, they should have drawn a blood culture."

"Stop, Stanley," Danielle commanded. She lifted Sarah's baby boy from the crib and cuddled him. "Just stop right now. We're doing the best we can."

"I'll ride in with her. Would you call Lavern and ask him to meet us in the ER?"

Doctor Lavern Smith stood at the ER entrance waiting, when the ambulance pulled into the ER bay alongside two critical care nurses. He recognized Sarah from the auto accident nine months previous.

"What the hell, Stan? What's wrong?"

"Five days post-partum…hemorrhaging, and I think septic. She collapsed and we found her lying on the floor, unconscious."

"Found her?"

"She showed up on our porch three nights ago…parents kicked her out…staying in our spare room."

"Unbelievable. Let's get her up to ICU."

The young night nurses stood on either side of the hospital hallway, staring as their barefooted, unshaven boss, wearing blue jeans and a bathrobe, and a rumpled Dr. Smith pushed the stretcher, carrying a very pale, blond girl with pink cheeks, down the hall and into ICU room 3. They all gathered around, and the team gently transferred Sarah into bed.

A custodian followed the stretcher with a mop, wiping away the bloody prints from Stanley's right foot.

The cardiac monitor showed a sinus tachycardia of 135. Her blood pressure registered a systolic pressure of 65 without a diastolic reading registered. A Foley catheter was inserted and no urine returned. Her body temperature registered 102.6.

"This looks serious." Everyone turned to see Dr. McCaferty standing at the entrance of the room, looking equally disheveled. "Danielle called me." He joined the team, working quietly, assessing, starting central IV lines, drawing blood specimens, and starting blood transfusions. At three forty a.m. Sarah stopped breathing. Dr. Smith intubated her, and a respirator began breathing for her.

At five a.m., Dr. McCaferty walked back from the lab with a preliminary lab finding of staphylococcus aureus septicemia. Clindamycin was added to the antibiotic regimen. When her blood pressure failed to respond to blood transfusions and IV fluids, immune globulin was added to the IVs running.

Danielle walked down the ICU hallway towards room 3 with a determined expression and angry eyes, a 6 day-old baby boy against her breast, wrapped in a blue receiving blanket. Her fellow nurses stepped aside. One young nurse touched her arm when she walked past. Danielle stopped for an instant. They watched tears form in each other's eyes.

She walked into the room. Everyone stopped as Danielle worked her way through the IV lines and respirator tubing.

Danielle placed the child on the bed next to his mother.

"Sarah needs to be with her son before she goes to heaven," she said, looking up, "for just a little while." She shot her husband the look, which he understood completely…no matter the repercussions, no matter the hospital rules….

Timothy and Carla stood with their three-year-old son, Charles Dwight, at the room entrance. A young staff nurse, new to the Intensive Care Unit, attempted to keep Carla and her son out of the unit until she saw Stanley looking in their direction and waving them in.

Chief of Police Larry Strait and his wife, Dawn, joined the group.

And then Pastor Katherine McGinnis and her husband, Doug, arrived. Kate walked past the assembly at the entrance and wiggled through those working to save Sarah. She leaned over the bed, reaching through the contraptions and tubing, and placed one hand on Sarah's forehead and the other on her baby son. Danielle leaned from the other side, placing her hands on Kate's.

"Lord, we sure don't understand any of this terrible night. All we know is that you love each of us. Please help our aching hearts to understand. Sarah loves you very much. Welcome her home and hold her tight." Kate's voice choked, and she stopped.

At nine twelve p.m., Sarah Phillips died from septic shock and multi-organ failure, twelve days after her eighteenth birthday.

Stanley closed the door to the room and sat next to her for a long time, alone. The nurses at the nurses' station could hear him talking from time to time, and they wondered. The Director of Nursing, Ramona, quietly opened the door at ten thirty and stood silently behind Stanley with her hands on his shoulders. Several times the nurses watching saw Ramona's hands shake as his chest heaved.

Then he came out and walked to his office next to the nurses' station. He called Sarah's parents.

"Mr. Phillips, this is Stanley McMillen at Big Bay General. Your daughter was admitted a short time ago in critical condition. I am sorry to tell you that Sarah has died."

"The wages of sin," was the response, and the line went dead.

***

"The first time I met Sarah, she was in the arms of Dr. McCaferty as he carried her from the smoking wreck just at the end of this very block, only nine months ago," Pastor Katherine Kennedy McGinnis said from the pulpit. The Big Bay Methodist Church was filled, and people stood outside on the steps as well. Many had been present nine months earlier for the funeral for a stranger from Avon, Ohio, by the name of Michelle when the horrific accident occurred on Carter Street. Now they gathered once again to grieve for another young life lost, regardless of the fact they had never met her, except for that one day when many of the men pushed hard against the smoking dump truck, keeping it from crushing the young girl, as those inside the wreck tried to save her.

A lone Mennonite sat in the very front pew—Sarah's maternal grandmother—wearing a white bonnet on her head, softly crying as she twisted a hankie.

"She stopped in my office almost every Saturday," Pastor Kate continued. "Sarah's strength actually inspired me. At her young age, she made hard choices that would be daunting for adults. She loved and she forgave without condition. And she loved the life she was bringing into the world."

Kate paused and took a deep breath and then another.

"She loved Jesus very much. The first time I saw her, she was in the arms of Jack McCaferty. Now I can see her in the arms of Jesus."

The church was silent.

Timothy's wife Carla and her friend, Miriam Roosevelt, stood alone in the choir loft. They sang *What A Friend We Have in Jesus* without accompaniment.

Chief Strait, Wayne, Doug, Timothy, Stanley, and Dr. McCaferty carried her casket down the aisle.

Chapter Four

A Voice in the Darkness

The Usual Suspects, as they liked to be called, were gathered around the southwest table at Poor Joe's, drinking coffee and devouring Dora's freshly baked cinnamon rolls, made only on weekends. There sat Pete, Wayne, Wendell, Ralph, Morris, and now Richard, when Doug came through the back door and walked down the hallway past the men's room, followed by his German Shepard, Malcolm.

"What's happening with the adoption?" Wendell asked.

"What name you guys gonna pick?" Dora inquired, as she pulled another sheet of sweet rolls from the oven.

Doug sat down and looked at the men who looked back at his gloomy eyes.

"Don't think there's going to be an adoption."

"The hell you say. What do ya mean?" Pete shot back.

"Judge Linsenmayer says Sarah's parents are claiming him as his next of kin, and that she thinks they will send him to a Mennonite boarding school or orphanage or some damn place like that."

"They can't do that," was the unanimous response.

"She says they can and will, just out of spite cuz we had the funeral for Sarah at the Methodist church."

"They didn't want anything to do with her…kicked her ass out, with her baby…kicked them out. What the hell?" Wendell almost shouted, now standing. "What the hell!"

Doug shrugged. "Kate and some of her law school buddies were talking last night, looking for precedents to take to Judge Linsenmayer."

"Thought your wife's a preacher," Richard said.

"Was a lawyer before she went to divinity school."

"Oh. Where do these Phillips live?"

Everyone at the table turned to look at Richard.

"On a farm six miles east of town. Why?" Wendell responded.

"Not far then," Richard replied, wiping away some tears that chronically drained from his right eye. He lowered that hand and Malcolm licked it.

***

The brown eggs had been gathered from the henhouse and the sky had been dark for about an hour and thirty minutes. The Phillips sat in the large living room, listening to a crusade on the Christian A.M. radio station, which came in better after dark. Mr. Phillips stared into the fireplace and poked at the burning logs, causing a shower of sparks which lit up the room, illuminated mostly by a single floor lamp next to Mrs. Phillips' chair.

"I love Jesus."

The voice came from the darkness behind Mr. Phillips' big, overstuffed chair.

Mrs. Phillips looked up from her knitting, terrified of the disfigured face with a glass eye staring at her without blinking.

Mr. Phillips froze, and then began fumbling for something with his right hand under the chair. He stopped when a cold hard object pressed against the back of his head.

"Both hands on your lap, Mr. Phillips."

He complied.

Richard walked around the brown overstuffed chair and into the light of the floor lamp. Mr. Phillips glared at him.

"I understand you have an objection to the adoption of Sarah's baby by Kate and Doug."

"He's our grandson, and we'll choose what's best for the boy," replied Mr. Phillips, his right hand inching off his lap.

"Keep your hands folded on your lap…maybe even fold them like you're praying. If I see that hand move again, I'll blow it off."

Richard removed a large caliber revolver from his jacket pocket.

Mrs. Phillips began to cry.

"I am a close friend to your daughter," Richard continued, sitting down at the coffee table, facing both of the Phillips. "I spoke with her last night. She would like very much for her child to become the son of Katherine and Doug. They'll love him."

Richard placed the revolver on the coffee table.

"You're a stark raving lunatic. Our Sarah is dead. You're a nut," Mr. Phillips said in derision.

"This isn't a discussion of my mental status, sir. I'm here at the request of your daughter to see this adoption through. And it will, I assure you."

"You'll be in jail tomorrow."

"My name is Richard Elmore Fortin. I tell you this because I am certain I will not be in jail tomorrow. What I can assure you is that the folks in Big Bay are either going to be shocked that you murdered your wife and then committed suicide, or rejoicing that you have granted permission for the adoption to proceed without objection. The choice is yours, Mr. and Mrs. Phillips. You have until midnight."

Richard wiped the drainage from his right cheek and looked at Mrs. Phillips.

Mrs. Phillips wept.

I'm so sorry, Sarah…I'm so sorry…I love you with all my

heart…I'm so sorry, my precious daughter…mommy loves you…

***

Kate was in her office at the rectory when she received the phone call from Judge Linsenmayer.

"Sarah's parents just left my chambers. They've had a change of heart, said it would be best for 'the boy' to be adopted by a loving couple…signed all the papers. You guys are going to have a son!"

"Oh, my. Thank you, Faith. Doug is going to be giddy. Thank you."

"God works in mysterious ways, pastor."

"Yes he does, judge."

***

Richard walked down the stairs Tuesday morning, followed by Wendell. "Any possibility we could have cinnamon rolls every morning?" he asked Dora.

"Nope," replied Dora as she nodded in the direction of the southwest table.

"Good morning, Richard."

Chief of Police Larry Strait sipped a cup of black coffee and smiled up at the stairs.

"Good morning, Chief."

"Have a complaint lodged by the Phillips, stating you threatened their lives," the chief said.

Richard walked towards him.

Wendell stopped partway down the staircase.

Dora carried two more cups of black coffee towards the table, precariously, spilling a trail, while staring at Richard.

"That sounds like something I would not likely do," Richard said, sitting down at Larry Strait's table, looking directly at the chief. "I'm

16

new in this town with no vested interest."

"Well, they wrote out a complaint, stating you violated the sanctity of their home this past Sunday evening, threatening them with a handgun before leaving at midnight."

"Did they mention why I'd do such a thing?"

"Vague on that particular subject. They were concerned you were going to rob them."

"Chief," Wendell said from the stairs.

The chief looked up to see Wendell, Pete, and Wayne standing on the stairwell landing and Timothy putting on an apron, with Dora tying it in the back.

"I'm not sure if maybe the Mennonites got some bad communion wine or something," Wendell continued slowly. "But us guys will swear Richard spent Sunday right here with us, playing Old Maid, from supper until about two."

"Mennonites don't drink," the chief shot back, looking from one person to the next.

"That we know of," Pete retorted.

"There you have it, Chief," Richard said, glancing up at the men, "What Wendell said."

"Yup," Chief Strait said, reaching for his coffee cup, "cinnamon rolls would be nice every morning, Dora."

Chapter Five
Little Miss

Poor Joe's old hardwood floor creaked with each tentative step. Machete Juarez walked behind a pale, Golden Retriever, past the men's room and his faded bloodstain, embedded in the wood. Timothy put his hand up. The dog stopped.

Machete stood at the entrance leading to the bar from the hallway, smiling a big smile, his head moving back and forth, listening, like a blind man looking around.

Carla enveloped Machete in her arms. He dropped the guide dog leash and wrapped Carla tightly with his arms. He took a deep breath and exclaimed, "Carla. I know your perfume!"

He patted her back with both hands, grinning over her shoulder.

The old bar was quietly packed, door-to-door. When Machete appeared, everyone erupted with hand clapping and then singing, *"For he's a jolly good fellow."*

For the past seven months, after surviving a gunshot to the head after entering the back door at Poor Joe's and being given no hope of survival, Machete had undergone rehabilitation in Rochester, Minnesota. Dr. McCaferty made the arrangements. Machete's friends, Vincent Bonifacio and Quinn O'Malley, arranged the flight from Big Bay to Rochester. When the strange looking black helicopter arrived at St

Mary's helipad, the staff had watched with fascination while a large, sleek machine without markings landed gently.

When the door lifted, a banner on the helicopter ceiling reading TRUE BELIEVERS, in large red letters, puzzled them.

Quinn and Vincent had paid the medical expenses.

And there he stood, surrounded by adoration from the patrons of Poor Joe's, the very bar he had been hired to burn down and the people he was sent to murder before he came over from the dark side.

"We've built a room for you!" Timothy exclaimed.

"Yeah," Wendell added, "it's right under the stairs."

"That's the storage room," Machete said.

"Not anymore," Wayne replied, "Just wait till you see it. Oops…sorry, you can't see. Damn…sorry."

The bar became quiet with embarrassment.

Machete grinned.

"I can see things better than you can ever imagine; watch yourselves!

The patrons roared with laughter and clapped.

"What's your dog's name?" Danielle asked.

"Little Miss. I named her Little Miss. We love each other."

Little Miss' white tail with a yellow tip wagged back and forth. She looked up at Machete with adoration.

Chapter Six

Two Strangers and Their Mongrel Dog

The United States marshals arrived in three black Suburbans and turned into the parking lot behind the Big Bay City Police Department. The marshals stood in a cluster, discussing something, and then four marshals left in one of the vehicles, headed towards downtown.

"Looking for Chief Strait," the lead marshal said to the desk sergeant in the dispatch room.

The seated sergeant looked up, studying the face of the burly man with a large sidearm on his right hip and the outstretched left hand holding a U.S. Marshal badge. He glanced through the window at the black vehicles.

"He'll see you now," the sergeant said, placing the phone in the cradle. "First door on the right."

Chief of Police Larry Strait looked up without his customary smile. He did not extend his hand or stand.

"Help you, Marshal?" He pushed the intercom button to the desk sergeant. The sergeant listened to the sounds coming through the little speaker on his desk.

The marshal pulled folded papers from his vest. He unfolded the crisp white papers and pushed them on the desk towards the chief. Larry Strait stared at a photo of Richard Elmore Fortin and a warrant for his arrest, authorized in Monroe County, Florida.

"Federal warrant for Richard Elmore Fortin, on the charge of espionage and failure to appear."

Chief Strait looked up without response.

"I need his location, Chief."

The chief shook his head slowly and answered, "You guys come back at six. He'll be here."

The phone rang several times at Poor Joe's before Timothy answered.

"Poor Joe's, Timothy speaking; Joe ain't here."

"Tim…Sergeant Akin here, Chief Strait would like you to know there are federal marshals in town with a warrant for Richard."

"What charge?"

"Espionage and jumping bond from Monroe County. Chief told them he would have Richard waiting for them here at the jail at six."

"Thanks…think they just arrived…bye."

Timothy watched a black GMC Suburban, with several little antennas protruding from the roof, drive slowly past the bar, then back up and turn into the parking lot. Quickly, Timothy reached under the counter and brought out a six cell, black flashlight.

"Richard!" he shouted at the men sitting around the southwest table. "Follow me!"

Timothy and Richard stopped at the door adjacent to the men's room door.

"This is the way to the basement," he said while he unlocked the door and opened it. "There are federal agents here to arrest you. At the bottom, turn right. On the far wall you'll see cases of beer stacked. Move the cases of Schlitz. There's a trap door…to an old tunnel used during prohibition; leads to the river."

Richard stared at Timothy.

"Nope, I've never been in the tunnel. That's what I've been told. Hurry."

He pushed Richard through the door and locked it.

The marshals entered through the front door and were greeted by Wendell, playing with the remains of his grenade-disfigured right hand, while looking the men directly in their eyes, first one and then the next marshal, without blinking even once.

"You guys thirsty?"

"Looking for Richard Elmore Fortin," the tall marshal replied, looking at the men sitting at the table. "Where is he?" The man produced a marshal's badge

"Ain't that pretty!" Wendell said. "Had one just like that in the 5th grade."

"You want to be arrested for obstruction?"

"Nope, I'm serious; got one for Christmas. Had a Daniel Boone outfit in the 4th grade."

The agent pushed Wendell to his left and the marshals walked towards the table, looking face to face.

"Where's Richard Fortin?"

Timothy slowly, quietly opened the squeaky door to the old phone booth in the hallway and closed it softy. He quickly dialed.

"O'Malley's Charter Service."

"Federal marshals here to arrest Richard, Quinn. What the hell?"

"Trumped up charges. We helped Fidel with a little problem— mutual aid thing—and the director is pissed we didn't get permission. I'm sorry, Timothy."

"Quinn, never apologize to me again; you saved my wife and son. What should we do now?

"Get him to the airport—the old hanger—after dark. We'll get'em out of the country. Thanks, Timothy."

Click.

Timothy called Carla.

"Carla, need your help right now. I need you to drive down to where Cass ends at the river. Go to the dock on our property; Richard will be coming out from a tunnel. Take him to the old airport. Keep him out of sight. Just drop him off and get home."

Several seconds of silence…

"I'm on it."

Timothy opened the phone booth door and stood face to face with a U.S. marshal glaring intently.

"Who you talking to?"

"Let me check," Timothy said, staring right back, eye to eye. "Oh, that's right, I'm in the United States of America, retired United States Army, honorably-discharged Green Beret with a Purple Heart for my efforts, and I don't have to tell you a damn thing, sir"

"I'll arrest you for obstruction."

"Since when is it a criminal offense to call my wife?"

"In a phone booth?"

"She's that kind of girl."

The marshal stepped back and looked at Timothy's right arm, which ended in a stump just above the elbow.

"Lose your arm in the war?"

"Nope, lost it during the rescue of my friend," Timothy replied, pointing towards Wendell. "We look out for each other."

The marshal nodded. "I still need Richard."

***

Richard pulled up on the trap door, hard as he could. The rusty metal ring slipped from his grip several times before the door moved. He pointed the flashlight into the black hole. A grungy metal ladder descended fifteen feet to brown water with floating slime.

He took a deep breath of air resembling rotting apricots, horse urine, sauerkraut, and death.

At the foot of the ladder, Richard stood ankle deep in the brackish fluid. Light colored bricks constructed the tunnel in an arched configuration, with the ceiling peak at least ten feet high. Shining the flashlight beam into the darkness, Richard estimated the tunnel to be three hundred yards long.

Dead rats floated here and there, bobbing about in the shadows. He walked carefully on the slippery brick floor towards the end.

The massive, wet, wooden door at the end would not budge; Richard moved the latch and pushed hard. It did not move at all. He backed up and ran at the unlatched door, hitting it with his shoulder. The force knocked the flashlight from his grip; it splashed into the brown water and went black.

...and he was in the dirt fort. He and his younger brother Jimmy dug deep that spring Saturday into the clay bank under the tall walnut tree behind the barn.

....JIMMY...JIMMY...JIMMY...only wet dirt covering them and blocking the entrance. No Jimmy, just dirt in the black darkness...

"Richard, are you there?" came a soft voice from the other side.

"Yes."

"I'm Carla. Timothy told me to meet you here."

"Can't get the door open."

"Two fishermen stopped to help. They just put a long post in the door latch. You push, they'll pull."

The massive, mossy, wooden door at least a foot thick, opened. Richard stepped out, his face covered with cobwebs, some sticking to his right eye, into the sunlight.

The two men washed their hands in the cold river water. One fellow turned and said, "Trout are biting this afternoon."

And the two strangers, wearing hip high waders, walked up river. A tan mongrel dog, part bloodhound, followed them into the mist coming from the spillway.

"I'm sure happy they came along when they did," Carla said. "I know I couldn't have budged that door. Didn't know fishing season had started."

"Fisherman, huh?" Richard replied.

"My car's right there," she said pointing. "Charles is sound asleep in his car seat."

"Be great to see him again."

***

Six o'clock had passed two hours ago. An angry lead marshal strutted into Poor Joe's with Chief Strait at his side. The marshals had been at the bar all day and were now eating hamburgers. They stood up.

"I want to know what the hell is going on, and I want to know where Richard Fortin is, right now, or I'll arrest every damn one of you. NOW!"

A distant percussive vibration grew progressively louder, to the level that the chop-chop-chopping sound caused whiskey bottles on the shelf behind the bar to rattle against the mirror.

The marshals bolted through the front door, looking up into the darkness, watching a black flying machine without lights of any sort, eclipse the shining stars as it moved away towards the north, at first slowly, in a teasing fashion, and then rapidly.

"Get me the FAA!" the lead marshal screamed into his portable radio.

"What do you mean, there's nothing on radar? I just saw the damn thing flying over Big Bay."

He listened to another reply and tossed the radio on the front seat of his Suburban.

"We'll be back," he said, pointing at Chief Strait and Timothy who were standing side by side.

***

Richard looked up at the TRUE BELIEVERS banner on the ceiling.

"I used to fly this machine," he said to the four men dressed entirely in black, except for a little golden lion on each left shirt cuff.

"Yes, you did, sir. I've heard you are the best," replied the man sitting on his right.

"Where're we headed?"

"Safe house on the Belcher Islands."

"The Canadians know we're coming?"

"Yes, sir."

Chapter Seven

Some Sort of Miracle

...fingernail polish remover...polish remover...acetone...warm acetone...

Danielle opened her eyes, eye to eye with Chloe standing next to the bed in the dim, blue light coming from the old clock radio, breathing feverish breaths in her mother's face.

"My throat burns like a fire and my eyeballs ache inside," the eight year old said.

Influenza scared Stanley. Both he and Danielle had caught it in 1998, and so had Chloe when she was six, and they had all been ill for two weeks.

Now a new strain of the virus had arrived.

Doctor McCaferty claimed it came to Big Bay with the ducks as they migrated. Most people blamed the new family living on Ladd Street who moved from Atlanta and were all sick when they moved in, before anyone else caught it.

Some called it the Pig Flu. Big Bay General Hospital was filled to capacity most days as people developed respiratory distress and pneumonia.

Dr. McCaferty caught it and couldn't see patients or make rounds for three weeks. All the residents at Poor Joe's came down with the aches, fever, and congestion, except for Dora and Machete. The Usual Suspects drank more than usual under the guise of medicinal purpose and never sought actual medical care.

Danielle had the flu first at the McMillen residence, blaming working in the ER. Stanley had it 5 days later and blamed himself for sleeping with a contagious person.

"Stanley, wake up. Chloe's sick."

"What?"

"I just took her temp...102.8."

"Shit. I'll get my stethoscope."

"She's congested all the way up, both sides," Stanley said, looking at his wife, listening to his daughter's lungs.

"Daddy, my skin hurts all over."

Danielle called Chloe's pediatrician

"Dr. Fox said he'll meet us in the ER."

They pushed through the congested, sick people standing and sitting in the Emergency waiting room, past the admissions desk, as the receptionist looked up with a halting look on her face. They walked, without stopping, towards the elevators, Stanley carrying his limp, wheezing child, burning-up with a bluish-colored complexion.

Dr. Fox walked quickly from behind and caught up with them. "Keep on going, Stan," he said, looking at Chloe on her father's shoulder, "to the Peds ICU."

Chloe became listless, to the degree that she did not object when blood specimens were drawn and IVs started and a little catheter placed in her bladder.

She stopped crying.

"Stan, Danielle, we need to support her on a ventilator," Dr. Fox said.

He pulled the couple close with his arms. "She's getting tired."

***

"My sister needs me," Machete said, walking from his room, following Little Miss. "Maria needs me."

The men sitting around the southwest table watched the little Mexican walk towards them.

"What's wrong?" Timothy asked from behind the bar.

Little Miss turned Machete around. "My sister is in the hospital. She needs me."

Timothy picked up the phone and called the McMillen residence. Then he called the director of nursing office,

"I'll take you to the hospital. Let's go." Timothy turned to The Usual Suspect's table. "Everybody start praying for Chloe."

Machete walked through the Emergency Room throng, his chin jutted out with determination, being led by a Golden Retriever. Timothy led them to an elevator and pushed the button to the third floor.

The procession entered the Pediatric ICU, past the nurse's station. Stanley raised his head off his daughter's torso and looked up as they entered the room.

"I'm here, precious sister."

Danielle began to sob.

Stanley stood up and directed Machete into his chair. Little Miss sat beside Machete, looking up.

"How'd he know?" Stanley whispered. Timothy shrugged and began to tremble, looking at the cyanotic little girl with a tube in her throat.

"I am here now, Maria; I am here and this time will be all right," he said in Spanish, reaching up, feeling for the little girl's face with the fingers of both hands.

…bang…bang…bang…rat-a-tat…tat…yellow street lamp shining through the new holes in the wall…red dripping from the crib…on mother's body…

Stanley pulled a chair next to Danielle and held her tight. He stared at their daughter.

Danielle sat with her eyes closed. She rested her head against Stanley, reliving the evening they gave life to this dream, this daughter she adored, before they traveled to Key West, before Captain O'Malley married them on his boat, *The Key West Dreamer*.

Stanley stared at his daughter lying on white sheets, intubated, and limp. The many times he had been on the other side of the bed, working to save another family's child, raced through his mind in kaleidoscopic flashes. Now he sat beside the bed. The anger of helplessness ebbed and flowed.

No one, for three days, left Chloe's bedside. Timothy took Little Miss for walks to relieve her self and to eat. Machete refused to leave, except to be led to the bathroom. The nurses brought him food from the cafeteria. The pediatric waiting room was now occupied by, The Usual Suspects. Poor Joe's closed. Katherine Kennedy McGinnis and her husband, Doug, joined the group as soon as they got the news. So did Chief Larry Strait and his wife, Dawn. And then Quinn O'Malley arrived from Key West. Timothy had called him.

Do you see them? Little Miss asked Machete, looking up at two angels resting on either side of Chloe's pillow.

I see them, Machete answered, without uttering a word. And he squeezed the little hand harder. It felt very hot.

A third angel floated through the ceiling and sat next to Machete's head, resting down on the mattress.

I know you, beautiful one. You are Janet Sue.

The angel smiled. *You remember.*

Little Miss watched Janet Sue intently.

Katherine Kennedy McGinnis stood in the waiting room. "We need to pray very hard right now, everybody. Just pray as hard as you know how." And then Katherine began to pray out loud, staring at the ceiling, with tears flowing.

"Lord, this time we ask you for a miracle. Please don't take this precious child home yet. We need her. Stanley and Danielle need her.

We all need the love that she brings to our lives, and we ask you to cure her of this awful virus. We love you Jesus. Please help us."

Katherine grasped the back of a chair to steady herself. Janet Sue stood immediately in front of her, face to face, smiling. *Your faith will be rewarded*, the angel said, and she was gone. Katherine trembled, every inch of her felt hot and twitchy. She sat down and gulped several times.

"Chloe's going to be ok…"

The men in the room stared at their pastor.

Doug smiled. "You saw her, didn't you? You just met Janet Sue." He bent down, hugging his wife.

Dr. Fox admitted it must have been "some sort of miracle." The helpless feeling, watching his friend's child's life dwindle away, had given him agony. Over the next 24 hours, Chloe's oxygen saturation improved back to 98%, and she was extubated the following evening. The fever broke and never returned. Urine began to trickle into the Foley bag.

Thank you, Machete said, looking eye to eye with Janet Sue.

Little Miss watched as Janet Sue and two other angels drifted away through the ceiling.

***

One week to the day she was admitted, Chloe Norma McMillen was discharged from the Pediatric Intensive Care Unit at Big Bay General Hospital.

"That was a close one," Stanley said to Danielle as they drove their daughter home.

"My heart was breaking. Couldn't believe this was happening to us," she replied, and she put her cheek on her husband's shoulder.

"Machete is something else."

"He was looking around the room like he could see someone."

"I think he did, Danielle."

"Machete can see angels," Chloe said from the back seat.

Chapter Eight

Nine Eleven

Even though their daughter had fully recovered from the terrible influenza without further complications, Stanley did not want to leave town. Every year for the past five years he and Dr. McCaferty had flown together to Washington D.C. and attended the week- long cardiology conference, titled TCT.

This year Dr. McCaferty had a conflict and could not attend. Stanley didn't want to go either, but the conference and plane tickets had been purchased. Stanley felt obliged not to waste Big Bay General's education budget.

10 a.m. on Sunday, Stanley felt Danielle's heart pounding through his shirt. They hugged goodbye at the airport. Danielle felt Stanley's heart pounding, too, his arms wrapped around her back and squeezing.

"See you next Sunday," Stanley muttered into his wife's ear. He kissed Chloe twice.

"I wish Mommy and I could go, too. We could go to the museums!"

"Next year, Chloe. You've already missed enough school. Maybe we can all go next year."

"Jeeze," Chloe said.

And, then he walked through the Northwest Airlines gate towards the DC-9.

Stanley skipped several incredibly boring sessions Monday, taking a taxi from the convention center to the Hard Rock Café for lunch, and then walked to the Ford Theater next door. He stared at the balcony where President Lincoln had been shot and spent the remainder of the afternoon absorbing the museum in the basement of Ford's Theater. The blood-soaked long coat the president wore that evening and the hate filled news clipping shocked Stanley. And the bed in the boarding house across the street—only long enough to accommodate a five foot six inch person. *Far cry from the drawings in the history books,* Stanley thought.

He made it back to the conference in time to listen to a presentation by two Swiss cardiologists showing a correlation between stress and disease.

Stanley fell asleep that Monday night on the couch, watching the weather channel lady talk about snow in North Dakota.

The sound of a jet liner flying over the convention center, whining like planes do with their wings flaps positioned down for landing, rattled the windows a little. The engines sounded loud, at full thrust. No one gave the high-pitched whining much thought, and it was gone. Reagan International was not far from the Convention Center.

"What should we do now?" the young cardiology resident said as Stanley walked out of the men's room.

The young lady's blue eyes were fixed on Stanley; her pupils dilated wide with fear. She held an open cell phone in her right hand.

"What do you mean?"

"Just talking to my mom in New York," the trembling young lady said. "They're bombing New York."

"Who's bombing New York?"

The resident shrugged, looking up. "The phone went dead."

Stanley's mind raced.

"Let's get the hell out of here," Stanley said, grabbing her by the arm. "Let's get away from the Convention Center."

"Why?"

"A feeling. If we're being bombed, this building filled with thousands of cardiologists would make a nice target. Come on."

Mobs of people swarmed the streets outside the Convention Center.

...Ants streaming from disturbed anthills...

Confused people plugged the streets in all directions. Fire engines, unable to drive through the streets obstructed by automobiles and pedestrians, navigated up the sidewalks at a crawling speed, sirens wailing, heading in the direction of smoke rising in the distance, their red lights flashing.

From every direction, the sound of sirens...

The police officer in the middle of the intersection at 9th Street and Mt. Vernon stood at least six foot, eight inches tall, looking over the heads, surrounded by people milling around in all directions. With the blond resident in tow, Stanley wiggled through the crowd to the tall policeman.

"What's happening?" Stanley shouted over the din and sirens, looking up into the bright morning sun.

"They're using airplanes as missiles to attack us. Hit the towers in New York. Just hit the Pentagon," the tall man with a military haircut answered, looking down. He turned away briefly, talking into the shoulder microphone of a portable radio.

He turned back and continued, "And, there are eight more planes coming."

Prickles, cold prickles, covered Stanley's body. Cold, quivering prickles.

The blond resident made a sucking, whimpering sound.

And then came the roar of jet engines, sudden and obliterating all other sounds. The tall policeman looked down with angry eyes and shrugged. His mind traveled home to his slender, longhaired wife, and how he adored her. They had waited until he returned from the war with Hussein to get married. He had not wanted to make her a widow.

...Chloe will have only vague memories. Stanley's mind skipped from one image to the next: vacations in Key West, Cuba, Castro and O'Malley, the guys, *Danielle...Danielle...Danielle...*

They looked up towards the roaring sound, which trailed far behind the low flying F18 fighter jets. Six gray jets, flying far ahead of the sound they created, peeled away from their tight formation and began to circle Washington D.C., protecting it.

"There ain't no more planes coming now, little buddy," the tall policeman said, grinning. He slapped Stanley on the back. "No sir, there ain't no more planes coming now." And he walked away into the swirling crowd.

Stanley and the young resident worked their way through the crowd, while sirens reached a crescendo and ebbed, over and over.

"Reminds me of a scene from the movie *Armageddon*," Stanley said when they reached an open space.

"I remember that," she answered. "The scene where the dog named Little Richard fell into the hole."

"That's the one. And the street scene in the movie *War of the Worlds*...this is surreal."

Military vehicles pushed through the crowd, being driven by men wearing green berets and sunglasses.

Yellow *DO NOT CROSS* tape soon encircled a large radius six blocks from the White House. And then each block progressively closer to the president's house was encircled, like the growth rings of a tree. Young men with automatic weapons stood at attention, ready to enforce the restrictions.

"I can't get back to my hotel," Stanley said in sudden recognition of his situation. "I'm at the Hotel Washington. I can't get back. I'm homeless."

The young cardiology resident extended her hand towards Stanley.

"My name is Eva. You can stay in my room. I'm at the Ritz-Carlton."

"Really?"

"I've got double beds." And she laughed." You can stay in my room, Stanley McMillen," she continued, looking at the convention credentials hanging around his neck. They walked for twenty minutes.

Mean looking, or scared, hotel security guards and a D.C. policeman stood at the entrance to the hotel, demanding identification and room number, comparing names given to the guest register.

"Eva Liljestrand," she said as they approached the entrance. "And this is my guest," she exclaimed with confidence, holding Stanley's credentials towards the peering security guys.

One security guard put his hand out to stop Stanley.

"He just arrived at our cardiology conference today," Eva said confidently to the pudgy man, looking him directly in the eyes, just a few inches from his face. "He is a colleague and he is staying with me. We're in room 443."

The fat man pulled back and waved them through the door with his plump fingers. "Next," he said, pointing at several terrified teenagers.

All day Tuesday Stanley tried to call Danielle, several times an hour. Every attempt was met with either a busy signal or no sound at all. After sunset, he lay on the bed next to the window, listening to jet fighters fly over the city, protecting it. Every thirty minutes he called Danielle using the bedside phone, without success. His cell phone remained useless. Eva dozed and read intermittently in the bed next to the television, turned on with the sound muted.

No easy way could be found out of Washington D.C. after the attack. The conference was cancelled Wednesday morning. Those who had driven to D.C. drove away. Those who could afford it purchased used cars, emptying the lots, and drove away. The rental cars had been snatched up in a matter of hours. The train schedule was booked for two weeks. Finally, a person answered the phone in the Greyhound office.

"No, sir, we ain't got no seats available until Friday."

"I need two seats: one ticket to Big Bay and one to New York

City."

"Best we can do is get youz both to the hub in Richmond and youz make your arrangements from there."

"Help me here. Please help us," Stanley replied.

A pause ensued, lasting at least 20 seconds, with fumbling paper sounds.

"Iz can get youz one ticket to Toledo…and one to Brooklyn. What be your credit card number?"

Stanley put the phone back in the cradle and turned to tell Eva when she wrapped her arms around him.

"Thank you, Stanley. I'm so scared. Thank you for walking out of the men's room when you did."

Stanley laughed. "Greyhound tickets on me, Eva."

Thursday morning while eating breakfast in the hotel restaurant, Stanley stopped mid-bite.

"I've got to get back to my hotel before we leave. All my stuff and presents and my new Hard Rock leather jacket…I've got to…"

"How you gonna manage that?" Eva asked between bites of a croissant.

"Don't know. Gotta try. Have a feeling I'll never see that stuff again if I don't go back. Walk with me to the first tape. If I get through, I'll meet you here tomorrow at 6 a.m. in the lobby."

Together they approached the first plastic barrier tape, yellow and flapping in the wind.

"Luck," she said

Eva squeezed Stanley's hand, hard.

Stanley approached the young man wearing sunglasses, holding an automatic rifle at the ready and no smile.

He approached the young soldier cautiously.

"Halt."

Stanley extended the official TCT identification badge from the lanyard around his neck and walked closer. The soldier peered at the ID while holding his rifle with both hands, reading, *Stanley James McMillen PhD RN TCT 2001 Big Bay General Hospital.*

He looked at Stanley, back at the credentials, then back at Stanley.

"Driver's License."

Stanley produced it from his wallet.

"What do you want?"

"I need to get to my hotel, Hotel Washington, to get my stuff before I leave for home tomorrow."

The young soldier studied Stanley through his dark sunglasses.

"What kind of stuff?"

"My clothes. Been wearing this suit since Tuesday."

"You go directly to the Hotel Washington, get your belongings, and come back. You understand?"

"Yes, sir."

The soldier lifted the yellow tape and Stanley ducked under it.

He walked the next block towards another yellow *DO NOT CROSS* tape, credentials dangling from the red lanyard around his neck. Each block for the next five blocks, Stanley approached the yellow tape and a young man holding a submachine gun and recited the same line, "The lieutenant gave me permission to get my stuff at the Hotel Washington," holding the TCT credentials at arm's length in their faces. Each guard nodded and lifted the barrier tape for Stanley to duck under.

In the hotel lobby, a mass of military personnel, wearing a variety of uniforms, milled around in a loosely formed line leading towards a long row of tables draped with white linen. Some men wore dark suits.

"Sergeant Major Wilden. How may I help you?" the stern man with a military haircut said, approaching Stanley.

Stanley extended his hand. "Sergeant Major, I was given permission to access my belongings on the seventh floor by Lieutenant Williams at the perimeter. I'm leaving town tomorrow."

They shook hands.

"He did, huh? Welcome to our smorgasbord," he said, pointing at the long tables covered with a variety of cold cuts and breads, as well as a man with a chef's hat carving prime rib and ham. "Get something to eat. And safe travels."

Stanley made two chicken sandwiches, smeared heavily with mustard, and took the elevator to the seventh floor. Sitting on his bed, he called Danielle.

She answered.

"Hi, Danielle."

He could hear her breathing, attempting to gain composure, breathing deep breaths.

"I've been so worried," she finally managed to say. "I heard about the plane hitting the first tower while I was driving to town and watched the second plane hit the tower on TV. And, then the news came that the Pentagon was hit, too. I've been trying to call you for three days. I love you."

"I've been trying, too. The phone lines are all congested...Great to hear your voice. If you've been calling my hotel room, I wasn't able to come back here after the attack until now; had a hell of a time getting back today. I'll tell you all about it when I get home."

"Where have you stayed?"

"Ritz-Carlton. A resident let me stay with her."

"Her?"

Stanley laughed. "Doctor Eva Liljestrand from New York City. She had an extra bed."

Danielle laughed. "Thank God somebody took you in. Lucky resident!

"Not even close, honey. I'm the lucky one, for sure."

"We're more than lucky."

"I know," Stanley replied. "I have Greyhound tickets to get out of D.C., taking me to Toledo, arriving on Monday."

"It's a date, honey. Chloe and I will pick you up Monday. I love you."

Outside of Richmond, the bus was pulled over by a state trooper and several black unmarked Ford Crown Victorias.

Men wearing bulletproof vests and one female with dark hair, wearing badges on their vests, entered the bus from the front door. Walking through the bus, each passenger was questioned as to country of origin, destination, and reason for travel. Then the bus was evacuated as the agents with bulletproof vests went through the luggage on board and then the luggage stored in the underbelly of the bus. A German Shepherd sniffed each suitcase before it was opened.

At 7:30 p.m. on Monday, September 17th, the Greyhound bus, which had originated in Washington D.C. three days earlier, arrived in Toledo, Ohio. Through the dirty bus window, Stanley saw Danielle standing under the roof of the arrival gate. Chloe stood beside her mom, looking in the mist like a little clone. The street and sidewalk glistened in the cold rain.

He clenched his jaws tightly, but his lips began to quiver.

Chapter Nine

The Reckoning

Little plaster craters remained in the white wall behind the great polished oak desk, unrepaired. Tiny flecks of blood, now dark with age, speckled the white paint around the three holes.

To the right, the shrine remained. Portraits of the godfather, Raul Veracruz, his son Diego, and Raul's grandson, Cesar Veracruz, hung in a cluster around a portrait of a beautiful Mexican lady. On a skinny ledge below the portraits, twelve candles, symbolizing the twelve apostles, flickered. Dark smoke shadows stained the white wall for several inches above each candle. The portraits had been rearranged, allowing for the addition of Cesar.

Jesus Veracruz sat behind his father's shiny desk, alone in the big office, surrounded by the tall walls of his family's compound in the Polanco area of Mexico City, staring at the portraits of his mother, father, older brother, and nephew. He ran his hand over the desktop, over the stains in the dark wood. Then he turned in the chair, twisting his neck to stare at the wounds in the wall behind him and the dark specks.

His mother had died when he was three, and Jesus could only remember her in his imagination. His grandmother raised him. He idolized his brother Diego, fifteen years his senior.

His grandmother told him at bedtime, his seven-year-old mind struggling to comprehend the news: his brother murdered by the City Police and Detective Timothy Fife in St Paul, Minnesota.

Now every morning, young Jesus drove alone through the wrought iron gates to his father's office. Every day he would light the twelve candles before sunrise, gaze at the three bullet holes in the white wall, and the dark flecks of blood that were his father's. Every morning he would swipe his hands over the dark stain embedded on the desktop where his father's head had rested.

And every morning he would stare at a single sheet of white paper lying on the dark bloodstain, reading the names handwritten on it, and the name of a whorehouse.

Every morning before sunrise, Jesus Veracruz sat at the desk where his father had been shot, gazing at the portraits illuminated by flickering yellow candlelight, and talked to them.

Some mornings the portraits spoke to Jesus, and he answered them.

***

The brothel, next to the five-star restaurant on the high hill overlooking Mexico City, had closed for the night. This had been Cesar's favorite whorehouse, the one he visited every Wednesday night, and the brothel he had visited the night he died in a car crash after the brake lines to his Mercedes had been severed.

The ladies were sleeping. Jesus picked the back door lock. He carried a basketball-sized bundle and placed it on the floor just inside, in a closet. At four thirty-five that Thursday morning, an explosion detonated, so violently that only the foundation remained of the cinder block building, the sound of it echoing down the hills for five miles.

Before sunrise that Thursday, Jesus lit the twelve candles, stared at the portraits, and then bowed his head.

"The reckoning has begun," he said out loud, raising his head from his hands, sitting in the chair behind the bloodstained desk.

"You are welcome, Pa Pa."

He crossed out the top name on the list using a number one pencil. The soft pencil lead made a wide mark.

Chapter Ten

A Leave of Absence

"**I** have a surprise for you," Danielle said, handing a package wrapped in a Cuban flag towards Stanley. He walked through their condo's front door. Her hazel eyes glistened with anticipation.

The oven timer rang.

"Wait…I've got a pie in the oven."

"What kind?"

"Apple brandy, your favorite."

Stanley walked out on the deck and plopped down in a white wicker chair, sighing with the exhaustion of yet another hard day at Big Bay General.

"OK…open it!"

"Can I open it? Let me open it, Daddy."

Stanley handed it to Chloe. "You open it."

Her parents watched their eight-year-old daughter gently unwrap the red, white, and blue flag with a single star, eventually revealing a medium pizza box. She handed it to her father.

Stanley stared down into the open box, which contained several CDs and a thin book titled, *Learn Spanish in Three Months,* and a legal-sized envelope with his name on it. He opened the envelope and felt his wife caressing his leg.

*Application for Leave of Absence...*Stanley read. Danielle had completed the form, requesting a three-month LOA, effective January first.

Danielle reached into her purse.

"I have one for you to fill out, too."

Stanley looked up at his wife standing next to his chair, her soul smiling back. They stared, just breathing, silent.

...We can't do this. It's too long to be away...

Her look melted him. She reached into the crack between the arm and the seat cushion, retrieving an envelope and tossing it playfully towards him.

The envelope contained two medical visas for Cuba.

"Whew!" Stanley finally uttered. "Cuba. You sure?"

"Honey, we've dreamed about this for over eight years, since our honeymoon." She paused.

"We need a change."

"Cuba...Cuba...Cuba," Chloe repeated excitedly, jumping up and down.

"When you were in D.C. and I couldn't get ahold of you, I thought *this is nuts, we have no promise of tomorrow.* We know *that* very well after all these years of doing what we do. Remember all those awful days in the ER, losing friends? I decided now is the time to live our dreams. We've lived through nightmares, honey: our Chloe being kidnapped; the bikers from New York shooting up Poor Joe's; Machete being shot and almost dying; Doug almost dying; Ric and Michelle murdered; Chloe almost dying. Just decided this is bullshit, honey. I want us to leave for a while and live our dream. What's the worst that can happen? Nothing that we haven't been through."

She stopped talking and put both hands on either side of Stanley's face.

"I'm all in, honey. Let's."

Danielle slipped her hands to his back. She squeezed his face into her breasts.

"MOTHER!" Chloe exclaimed.

"Dr. Gonzales says they need help setting up a clinic in a little town called Vinales. The old doctor there has Alzheimer's, and his nurse really never was one."

"I bet you've got logistics all worked out," Stanley smiled.

"Nope, but Quinn O'Malley is on it."

"Cuba!" Chloe said. "Where is Cuba?"

Chapter Eleven

Deep Gray Ache

Hugging her dying daughter being kept alive by a ventilator, feeling her precious body hot with fever had changed Danielle. The girl raised in *The Big Easy,* with a devil-may-care, but not me, spirit, now had a gray, deep ache in her soul. Her frequent flippant response, "What's the worst that could happen?" had now been answered by the reality of nearly losing part of her very soul.

She had stared at death, and she hated it.

Now lying next to her sleeping husband, she reached under the bed sheets and gently held his hand, her mind randomly jumping from thought to thought, reliving devastating memories.

...the time we met Dr. A.W. Blue, a man with a heart full of wisdom...showed me that things are seldom as they seem. And now he is missing off the coast of Cuba...

...the time Doug nearly died with a massive heart attack and cardiac arrest; now limping through life with courage...How Katie lives with this uncertainty amazes me...

...the time Chief of Police Charley Johnson got shot by the junkie in front of Lisa's Meat Market. We worked so hard to save his life, but he died...Timothy and Norma walking into that ICU room, hand in hand...

...the young clerk named Sara died that same day, shot by the same

junkie during a holdup. We couldn't save her either...Grandmother's now raising Sara's daughter...

...when Norma Jean died from lung cancer, smoking cigarettes to the very end, "because I like them," left Stanley depressed for months...our baby's middle name...Norma...

...September eleventh, the evil ones killed thousands of innocent people...starting the day in their offices, expecting to go home that evening...the poor people on those planes...tired to the bone...couldn't reach him...just blocks from the smashed Pentagon...three days sick inside; just sick...

...she was so hot when I hugged her little body...

...can only imagine how Carla felt...kidnapped and taken to Mexico City...Standing in front of that Mexican godfather, threatening to mutilate her baby in front of her...

...my parents' divorce...I was Chloe's age. Mother left with a man I never met. Now Dad's dead...adored him...He would come to every beauty pageant when I ran for Miss America...still see his beaming smile from the front row seat...

Danielle's mind skipped on the scratched record of her memories, jumping about.

...curly haired cousin, Joey, two grades ahead of me...wrote me beautiful poetry...found by a search party three days after his mom discovered a note on his pillow...they said he lay face down in the tall weeds next to a creek that empties into Lake Pontchartrain. Joey put a pistol in his mouth and pulled the trigger...just seventeen...couldn't go to his funeral...

Stanley squeezed Danielle's hand.

"It was a miracle, honey," he said to her in the darkness.

"What?"

"Kate and Machete told me."

"How'd they know?

"Remember the story Doug told us about Vietnam, when an angel hugged him during that terrible ambush? And, then he said he saw her sitting beside him in CCU after the cardiac arrest?"

"So?"

"Both Kate and Machete saw her sitting next to Chloe."

Danielle rolled over, putting her arm on Stanley.

"Machete is blind."

They lay side by side, listening to the grandfather clock tictocking in the other room.

"I've never believed in all that crap. I just never believed. Maybe now…I just don't know, honey."

Stanley kissed her. "Still want to go to Cuba?"

"Damn right."

Stanley had fallen asleep for about thirty minutes and was gently snoring when Janet Sue walked through the open bedroom door, holding Chloe's hand.

"I am happy to meet you, Danielle," the angel said with a voice reminiscent of wind.

"You have no idea what this means," Danielle replied.

"You say something?" Stanley said, rolling on his back and then feeling Chloe between them.

"Nope. Must have been dreaming," she replied.

The gray feeling evaporated.

Chapter Twelve

Blind Marksman

The Wednesday poker night started precisely at eight, as always, Timothy, Pete, Wayne, Ralph, Kate, Doug, Wendell, Morris, Stanley, and Jack McCaferty surrounded the long table in front of Poor Joe's kitchen area. Machete sat at the end with Little Miss to "watch" for any cheating. Dora had left for the evening. The new assistant cook/ dishwasher stared as he cleaned.

Jesus Veracruz had walked into Poor Joe's three weeks previously with the *HELP WANTED* sign, which had been stapled to the front screen door, in his hands. He had driven around the block past the old bar daily for eleven days, watching people come and go, studying faces. Sometimes after dark he would park in the alley off Grant Street and watch.

The day the *HELP WANTED* sign appeared on the front door, Jesus exclaimed, "Thank you, Pa Pa!" and he applied for the job helping Dora in the kitchen.

"Deal me in," Machete said, part way through the game.

Chuckles all around.

Jesus Veracruz watched.

"No cards for me," Machete continued. Jesus squinted at the blind man holding the cards.

The poker game concluded at ten pm, as usual. Machete did not win a single hand. "That was fun," he exclaimed. Everyone in the room laughed, except the new cook.

"Look out next week," he said, following Little Miss towards his room under the stair well. "I'm just playing games with your minds."

Jesus watched intently while he cleaned the counters and scrubbed frying pans, memorizing each face with a name on his list. He watched Machete with disdain, waiting to learn his name. No one had called the blind man by his name yet. *What a fool*, he thought, as he scrubbed the grill with a pumice stone. He watched Wayne, Ralph, Morris, Pete, and Wendell walk up the stairs to their rooms. Timothy took the money out of the cash register and walked out with Kate and Doug. Dr. McCaferty said goodnight to Jesus and left.

Jesus turned the lights off and left through the front door, which was never locked. At three twenty-three a.m., he returned to his Grant Street hiding place and parked. He opened the rental car's trunk and removed a heavy brown cardboard box. He walked softly and quickly through the dark alleys, avoiding the light from the street lamps as best he could. Silently, he entered Poor Joe's through the front door.

He set the box on the long table and lifted a large bundle wrapped with silver duct tape and a fuse extending from the center. Jesus worked quickly, uncoiling a long fuse towards the front door in the dim neon light coming from the Schlitz beer clock over the bar. He pushed the silver bundle on the floor to recess under the cash register.

"I see you prefer to do what you do in the darkness, as do I." Machete spoke in Spanish.

Jesus whirled back towards the sound of Machete's voice.

Machete stood at the end of the bar, Little Miss at his side.

Jesus said nothing, watching Machete, his head facing down in the direction of Little Miss.

Machete held a double-barreled twelve-gauge shotgun, pointing it in the general direction of Jesus.

Jesus moved first to his left a few feet and then to his right, watching Machete. Little Miss followed the movement with her head. The shotgun also followed his movements to the left and right.

"You should not want to hurt these good people," Machete continued in Spanish. "I once had that assignment, Amigo. My mind shudders when I think of the evil I had planned. I am thankful it did not happen. They are good friends."

"These are the pigs that have destroyed my family," Jesus finally spoke. "Pa Pa says I must."

"I am the one who destroyed your family," Machete said. "My name is Machete Juarez from Mexico City. I am the one who cut the brake lines on Cesar's Mercedes."

Jesus studied Machete, watching the shotgun move as Little Miss followed his movements.

"I think I will shoot your damn dog," Jesus said, drawing a handgun from his belt.

The very last thing that Jesus Veracruz heard was a single bark.

BOOM…BOOM…as the double barrel spewed buckshot. Brittle century-old glass tinkled crisply on the cement sidewalk outside, and then a dull thud.

Wendell, Morris, Ralph, Pete, and Wayne stood at the top of the stairs in their briefs. Wendell held a Luger pistol in his left hand. The dim light of the neon clock revealed Machete and Little Miss, sitting on the floor next to an object wrapped in silver tape. Little Miss licked Machete's face as he felt the bundle. A double-barreled shotgun leaned against the bar.

Pete flipped the light switch on.

"It's a bomb," Machete said, listening to the men approach.

Wendell reached down and yanked the fuse.

Pete and Wayne walked cautiously towards the man sprawled on his back near the front door in a growing pool of blood.

"Don't need no ambulance," Wayne muttered, looking back at

Machete's shotgun. He found no pulse on the dead man.

"Shit, it's the new guy, Dora's helper!" Pete exclaimed. "What the hell?"

The men stared at each other, remembering, without a word, the meeting with Cesar Veracruz and his grandson in Cuba.

"Chief Strait is on his way," Wendell said, hanging up the bar phone.

He was there in six minutes.

The chief pulled on rubber gloves and began going through the dead man's pockets. He opened the wallet and found eight, one hundred-dollar bills, a Mexican driver's license, and nothing else.

"Jesus Ramirez Veracruz: D.O.B. 3/3/1979."

"He is the youngest son of the godfather," Machete said.

From the dead man's shirt pocket Chief Strait carefully removed a folded white paper, a single hole through it, and the bottom saturated with blood. He gently unfolded the soggy sheet, spreading it out on the poker table. The men gathered around and read the list.

Palor masaje y placer palacio. There was a dark line drawn through it.

Fidel Castro…Cuba

Captain Quinn O'Malley…Key West

Timothy Fife…Big Bay

Stanley McMillen…Big Bay

Pete?…Big Bay

Wayne Collins…Big Bay

Vincent Bonifacio…St Paul

Chief of Police Strait…Big Bay

Machete Juarez…Big Bay

The men were staring at the list when Timothy, awakened at home by the motion-triggered alarm, opened the remains of the front door, stepped around the little lake of blood, and walked in, holding a revolver in his hand. He stared at Machete sitting on the floor, a shotgun leaning against the bar behind him, and a bundle of dynamite wrapped with silver duct tape. He followed the fuse now ending in the lake of blood.

Little Miss licked Machete's hand while studying the face of each man in the room.

Timothy shuddered, realizing he had hired the dead man.

"Machete shot him," Wendell said, pointing towards the shotgun. There was a hint of pride in his voice.

"Where'd he get it?" Chief Strait asked.

"I gave it to him. It was my father's," Timothy replied.

"You gave a blind man a shotgun?"

"I did."

Machete let out a little laugh. "You guys be more careful on poker night," he said with a grin while patting the bomb.

"OK. Let's get the coroner here. I need to talk with you, Machete. Down to my office."

Timothy and The Usual Suspects looked at the shattered windows, the front door hanging sideways on one hinge, and yet another bloodstain in the old hardwood floor.

"Guess we'll be closed today," Timothy said with disgust. "Damn it!"

The coroner arrived, spoke briefly with Chief Strait, and called for a hearse.

As Chief Strait, followed by Little Miss and Machete, walked towards the back entrance down the narrow hallway, Pete shouted, "On poker night, you leave Little Miss in your room, Machete!"

Machete laughed.

"This is the place I was shot," he said as they passed the men's room.

"I remember," Chief Strait replied.

"I am sorry that boy died," Machete said, walking out the back door.

Chapter Thirteen

Red Circle White Circle

Twenty-three boys stood in a circle, like high school boys do, trying to be men. In the center of the circle were two seventeen-year-old boys. The tall boy strutted about, talking trash about how he was going to pound the shorter boy into the ground. The tall boy's name was Charley Leach. The shorter boy, who stood 5'10", simply stared intently into the moving tall boy's eyes. The shorter boy's name: Richard Elmore Fortin.

Richard Fortin worked on his father's dairy farm when not attending school. Morning chores before catching the yellow school bus sometimes left faint smells of dairy barn clinging to his clothing. Charley walked past Richard between classes, making mooing sounds and sometimes squealing like a pig. Charley was a doctor's son with a high opinion of himself, and a feared bully. Given an opportunity, Charley would elbow Richard when they passed in the hallway, or bump into him, slamming Richard into the metal lockers lining the hallways, making the cluck-clucking sounds of a chicken, and walk away, flapping his arms like wings.

Suspended from the long wooden beam in the barn, by a twenty foot rope, hung a fifty pound brown burlap bag stuffed with a mixture of oats and straw. Two, six inch circles were painted on the bag—one barn red, and one white, just below the red circle and to the right.

Every evening, after chores were completed, Richard would give the bag a push, sparing with the moving target, hitting the circles with combination punches. He did this every night and had for over a year since Charley had commenced picking on him in the 10th grade.

The boys in the circle began chanting, "Fight…fight…fight." Charley Leach, without warning, hit Richard on the nose with his long, left arm. Blood splattered on Richard's face. The boys in the circle chanted louder.

A smile formed on Richard's bloody face. He stood still with his arms at his side.

"Is that all you got, Charley? Best you have?"

Charley lunged with fury, swinging wildly, his eyes large and angry.

Richard danced to the side and ducked back. Charley's wild punches glanced off Richard's arms. And then he straightened up and, with precision, hit Charley Leach on the jaw, followed by a blow to the sternum…*red circle…white circle*, and he smiled.

Charley slumped backwards, staggering, before he fell to the ground, his tall body stretched out on his back, unconscious for a few seconds.

The chanting stopped.

The circle of boys parted for Richard, wiping his nose, as he walked through it and towards the high school on the other side of the fence.

He stopped and turned when Charley shouted a brave obscenity while getting to his feet. Richard looked without saying a word. He pointed towards the ground, and Charley sat down.

Richard continued to spar with the stuffed gunny bag every day until he joined the United States Air Force two years later. Charley Leach never said another word to Richard. Charley avoided all eye contact and changed classes to avoid being in the same room.

More than anything else, Richard wanted to be an Air Force

helicopter pilot. While milking the cows, he dreamed of flying those machines. Driving the John Deere, he would close his eyes and imagine the sounds and bumps to be those of a flying machine.

His high school principal had written him a letter of recommendation. His history teacher also wrote a letter, mentioning Richard's leadership skills and good moral character.

The principal happened to be close friends with one of the U.S. senators from the state. Senator Griffith wrote a letter of nomination for Richard Elmore Fortin to the United States Air Force Academy.

At age nineteen, Richard was accepted. With unbridled enthusiasm, he traveled to Colorado Springs.

The fitness assessments for strength and agility were simply a quiz for the farm boy, breaking pull-up and sit-up records and running the mile in 5 min. 8 sec.

"Let's see how you do in wrestling," the examiner smirked during Basic Cadet Training.

"Yes, sir. I do prefer boxing, sir"

"Is that right, son?" And he blew his whistle.

"Mr. Fortin here tells me he would prefer to box." He walked over to a locker and then came back with two sets of boxing gloves. He tossed one set towards Richard and then walked over to a muscular black cadet.

"Let's see how you do against Mr. Fuller, Ohio State Golden Gloves Heavy Weight Champion."

The cadets stood in a square. The whistle blew.

The first blow moved Richards's body to the side several inches. The second blow came right though his guard, on the chin.

Nothing would move for a few seconds.

...fresh cut alfalfa...with a bitter, iron taste...keep pushing the bag...make little sister proud...Marie...on the beam, legs dangling down even though Dad spanks her for crawling up there...clapping and cheering...faster...faster...faster...Marie squealed...here it comes...red circle...left hand...white circle...hard right

The room was filled with stunned silence.

The heavy weight champion of Ohio sprawled unconscious on the gymnasium floor.

Four years of military and strategic studies, with a minor in Spanish, went by quickly. Richard became a commissioned officer, second lieutenant, at age twenty-three. His parents, being Quaker, did not come to the graduation ceremonies. His sister did not come either. She had died in an automobile accident when she was fifteen.

Flight training thrilled Richard in a liberating way. He became part of the flying machines when the rotors began to turn. His flight instructors watched him, while flying complex maneuvers, his face grinning from ear to ear.

"He has a flying instinct unmatched in my experience," his instructor said to the base commander. "Fortin becomes part of the machine; he's the brain for a living machine when he flies."

"Is he reckless?"

"No, sir. He would not want to hurt his machine. He is just very good."

"Let's put him in the new UH-60 Black Hawk."

Richard advanced over the coming years to Group Captain and was anticipating promotion to Wing Commander when it happened.

Flying low in formation with two other Blackhawks just off the shoreline of Honduras, a rocket-propelled grenade launched from the thick jungle hit the tail rotor of Richard's machine, blowing it away.

The sun was in his eyes and then it wasn't, and then again, over and over as the broken flying machine with the name *Marie* painted on the nose, spiraled downward.

…the heavyweight boxer from Ohio hit him again, and he clinched the big man, trying to hold on and clear his thinking…Little sister was hugging him tight now, around his neck, kissing his ear over and over…and the smell of fresh cut alfalfa…

He could hear them talking as they looked through his papers, looking for his blood type and calling the operating room.

...the smell of fresh cut alfalfa, again...and a roar before silence...

The pain in his right leg, held in a sling suspended from the apparatus above his bed, hurt white hot—more than the time that same leg had been pinched between the hay wagon and the granary and his eight year old sister pulled the wagon away, driving the Ford Tractor for the first time.

"You are a fortunate fellow," the nurse said, checking his blood pressure. "They were able to save your leg. Vascular surgeon reconnected most of the arteries."

"Hurts."

"That's good, Richard. I'll keep you comfortable. You've got rods in your femur, tibia, and fibula. Your x-ray looks like a hardware store."

"Show me."

She did.

After three months of rehabilitation at the Tory Pines V.A. Hospital in St. Petersburg, Florida, Richard had healed physically.

Nightly, he relived the groaning of his broken flying machine as it ricocheted through his mind.

...the ruptured tail section with its rotator still turning, flying in front, leading the way towards the ground...The sun coming and going and the smell of fresh cut alfalfa...Marie hugging his neck as they hit the ground together...

Richard told no one.

"Time to get out of this place and try your wings," Wing Commander Stanton said, walking into the hospital solarium, looking at Richard reading a newspaper.

"Yes, sir."

"Road trip up to Eglin. Get your stuff. Discharge papers are signed."

The following Tuesday they walked side by side towards a Blackhawk helicopter at Eglin Air Force Base near Valparaiso.

Richard climbed in, buckled the belts, plugged into the communications port, and reached for the switches to start the turbines. He noticed his fingers shaking while he flipped the switches. So did the wing commander.

The turbines started. Intestinal cramps bent Richard forward. He forced himself back into the seat. Commander Stanton watched Richard's ashen face.

"I think I've got the stomach flu," Richard exclaimed, unbuckling the seat belts and opening the door. The commander powered the turbines off.

…the sun swirling around and around… Little Marie hugged his neck and he braced for the crash…

***

"I recommend you take a Military Medical Retirement," Base Commander Lincoln said from behind his shiny desk with a little American flag on the corner. Wing Commander Stanton nodded in agreement and added, "You'll do better than with V.A. Disability."

For three weeks he had attempted to fly. Richard had tried. Each time he heard the whine of the turbines; each time he felt the chop chopping of the rotators; he experienced agonizing intestinal cramping. Each time his mind relived the machine he loved rolling over; each time he watched the tail section blown away, falling towards the ground even though he was staring straight ahead.

Richard could not fly the machines he loved.

He slumped forward and rubbed his scared right leg, itching at the scars.

"Yes, sir," he answered. "Can you have someone drive me to Key West?"

"Key West?"

"I need to get away from the world."

***

The farm boy from Iowa purchased a little house on White Street, a few blocks from Fausto's Food Palace grocery store. The house had a swimming pool, and swimming seemed to ease the ache in his right leg. Every morning he walked a few blocks to Sandy's Cuban Café for café con leche and a breakfast sandwich. At 1 p.m., precisely, Richard walked into El Siboney Restaurant, every day. They soon had his daily lunch of Puerco Asado ready as he walked to his reserved table. He tipped ten dollars for a ten dollar and seventy-five cent meal.

His favorite waitress was named Maria.

It took Richard nearly thirty minutes to walk from his house to Green Parrot Bar on Whitehead Street. The walk made his leg ache more, and he didn't care. He had a customary place at the bar, and the usual patrons knew him by name.

He watched with interest the tall man with curly gray hair and a Hemingway beard who, without fail, sat at a tall table on the Southard Street side, next to a window always open. The man arrived at 7 p.m. each day he came, just after Richard. The staff had a tall glass waiting for the man who, when he smiled, showed a missing front tooth. At 7:30 each evening, a waitress from the barbeque place next door would walk over, bringing a rack of ribs and slaw. They would flirt. He would ask her what time she got off work. She always said at midnight, and he would invite her to stop at slip 8. They would laugh.

The curly-haired man would leave the Green Parrot each night at 11: 30, walking in the direction of the marina. Three weeks after moving to Key West, Richard followed him in the darkness.

The man was sitting on the deck of a boat named The Key West Dreamer, smoking a cigar and drinking from a tall glass, when Richard came around the corner by the Conch Republic Seafood Company.

"You following me for any particular reason?" the man asked, looking up from the boat.

"I don't know."

"You don't know if you are following me, or you don't know if you have a reason?"

Richard stared down at the man smoking a Cuban cigar.

"Why don't you come aboard and introduce yourself properly, Richard Elmore Fortin."

Richard smiled. He climbed down and extended his hand.

"You've done some homework."

"Been watching you at the Parrot. Like to know the people watching me."

The man grinned, shaking Richard's hand.

"Captain Quinn O'Malley. I have a little charter service—no fishing. Have a seat."

The captain went below briefly, returning with a manila folder. He opened it.

"Let's see…says you are medically retired Air Force, shot down over Honduras while flying reconnaissance in a Blackhawk named for your late sister, that your right leg is mostly metal and mostly healed, and you suffer from the trauma of being shot down and you can't fly now. That about sums it up, Group Captain Fortin?"

Richard nodded and replied, "Charter boat captain, my ass."

Quinn O'Malley laughed.

"Honest, there's my license," he said, pointing.

He continued, "I've got a friend who needs a good chopper pilot, sophisticated machines right down your alley."

Richard played along.

"Which machine?"

"X-S 1. Built for us by the Germans. Constructed of composite. Stealth and fly a bit faster."

"How fast?"

"Four hundred miles per hour. Three man cockpits. Looks like the inside of the old Apollo space capsule: pilot, copilot, and navigator…room for twelve in the back. She's wide, flat, fast, and invisible to radar. Thrusters make maneuvering a dream. She's a beautiful machine, and we're going to get you in one."

"What you drinking, Captain?"

"Mount Gay Rum, the only thing worth drinking."

"I think you've had too much."

"That's yet to happen, young man. Tomorrow you and I are going over to the airport and borrow a friend's biplane."

"Why?"

"So you can let the air blow your hair back and so you can talk it over with your little sister."

Richard shivered and nodded.

"You have another glass?"

"I'll do the flying," Quinn said. He poured Richard a full, tall glass.

Chapter Fourteen

The Sound of Colors

Danielle and Carla sat on the condo deck, looking at the city of Big Bay in the valley below, talking before their children got out of school.

"Steve Chase started calling me again," Danielle said.

"Oh jeez. What'd you tell him?"

"Nothing. I answer the phone and he says, 'I still love you,' and hangs up."

"Have you told Stanley?"

"Not yet."

The friends paused and looked down the hill.

""How long you guys go together?"

"Since eighth grade, through college. A long time."

"I promised Timothy…oh to hell with it…Steve Chase came to Big Bay after you broke off the engagement, looking for Stanley. Timothy told me he stormed into Poor Joe's asking for Stanley. The guys all told him to go home, and then called Stan. They had a fight in the middle of the bar, Danielle. Stanley knocked Steve out."

"Glad you didn't tell me. Now I'm scared," Danielle said. "Let's go pick up the kids. It's almost three. I feel sick."

***

Steve Chase hated everything about Big Bay. He hated the men at Poor Joe's who jeered at him, lying on the floor after being knocked out, standing over him waving white bar towels at him. He hated the bar owner and the drunken fools who lived there. Mostly, he hated the man married to the woman he loved. He hated Stanley McMillen.

In his garage, tucked in the back of the screwdriver drawer, Steve kept a small metal toolbox with a clasp secured by a combination lock. Danielle's birthdate opened the combination.

Most every evening after dinner, while his wife cleaned the kitchen and made sure the children were doing their homework, Steve would go to the garage to "tinker." Using his old lover's birthday date, he opened the red metal box in a ceremonial fashion. He would handle carefully each photograph: pictures of them together in the eighth grade, then high school, then graduation and college pictures, ending with the Polaroid of his only love standing on the beach in front of a Christmas palm with little red seeds strewn on the white beach sand, naked, and smiling back at him.

...if that Stanley McMillen never existed...Wish I hadn't pushed her to get married...if I'd gone a little slower...if that bastard didn't exist...if she'd said yes, everything would have been perfect...

"I have to take a trip to Boston," he told the family during supper on a Monday evening.

"Why?" asked his wife.

"Problem with a contract, better dealt with face to face. I'll only be gone a couple of days."

***

Stanley missed the poker night at Poor Joe's that Wednesday. Doctor McCaferty stayed late at the hospital, too.

Tiffany Hannah moved from Ann Arbor, Michigan, to live with her mother in Big Bay. She drove her three children back to her hometown the morning after her husband hit her.

"A dream coming true," she had told her best friend, following the marriage proposal from the dark-haired Emergency Room physician from Mayo Clinic. "I could not be more thrilled."

They had met at the hospital, she as a registered nurse from the University of Michigan with a master's degree, Jon was a third shift ER doctor. His parents, from La Jolla, California, paid for the wedding and honeymoon on Maui.

It started after their first baby.

"How long you gonna have that baby fat?" Jon would chide, whacking at the soft parts, roughly.

"You see the new crop of nursing students on ER rotation? Some real lookers," he said one evening as she changed their third baby's diapers.

"Which ones?" Tiffany shot back. "And where were you last night?"

"What?"

"Which ones? Guys or girls?"

The punch to her stomach crumpled Tiffany. She dropped their baby on the carpet, curling on the floor beside the little girl, gasping for air.

Jon slammed the door. Tiffany listened to his Porsche squeal from the driveway.

She quivered on the floor, facing her crying five-month-old daughter.

...Prom night...Teddy gently touching me, his eyes wide with questions and I said yes with my eyes for the first time...had to go to U of M...poor Teddy...wonder if he's still working in his daddy's garage...he was so kind...

The director of nurses hired Tiffany for the Big Bay ER night shift following one phone call. "She was nurse of the year in Ann Arbor two years ago," she said to Stanley during lunch in the cafeteria.

Third shift worked well for Tiffany. Her mother watched the children and had the two older children ready for school before Tiffany arrived home from work.

Wednesday morning. The yellow bus was driving away in the distance when she arrived home.

...Damn. I wanted to hug them...

Tiffany and her mom were sitting at the kitchen table eating cheesy scrambled eggs on English muffins when Jon opened the front door, slamming it against the wall. He grabbed Tiffany by the arm.

Her mother hit the big man with a greasy cast iron frying pan. He knocked her down with a single blow.

Tiffany bit him, clawing and terrified. He dragged her through the front door. The blue scrub top ripped partly away. Jon threw his wife like a bale of hay to the sod. She covered her head with her arms, lying on the ground while he kicked her in the belly, chest, and repeatedly in the face. Her screams became gurgles.

Chief Strait answered the 911 call from Tiffany's mother. Climbing from the patrol car, the horror of what his stunned mind witnessed sickened the old war vet. He ran towards the horror with his service revolver drawn. The curly-haired man stopped kicking his wife and charged Larry Strait, the morning sun shining in his wide, furious eyes.

...the F4 wreckage was strewn all around in the palm trees, and burning...the Vietcong yelling in the jungle, coming closer...stand up and fight...and fired his sidearm...

A single shot hit the attacker in the middle of his broad forehead.

The chief walked past him without looking. He scooped Tiffany from the ground and walked back to the patrol car. Gently, carefully, he put the unconscious nurse on the back seat.

He radioed the Emergency Room.

Squadron Leader Larry Strait flew his F4 fighter very close to the ground all the way to the Big Bay ER.

Stanley and Ramona joined the ER staff, working to save one of their own. Tiffany's face was swollen beyond recognition, her uniform ripped, and name badge bloody. They worked with determination, doing what they do, refusing to surrender to evil. Dr. McCaferty did an echocardiogram and then a pericardialcentesis to remove blood accumulating in the sac around her heart. Dr. Smith intubated her. Dr. Varner arrived from home twenty-three minutes later, ignoring the state police chasing his speeding sports car.

They worked on their friend all day, trying to stabilize her enough for exploratory surgery. Despite transfusions, IV fluids, and vasopressors, Tiffany's systolic pressure lingered in the low 60's. What little urine formed in the Foley bag was bloody. A head CT at noon found no evidence of bleeding in the brain.

"She's all busted up inside," Stanley said quietly. He suctioned continuously the bloody froth from the endotracheal tube. He put his hand on Tiffany's swollen forehead and closed his eyes.

At 9 p.m., Dr. Varner said, "She's gone; she's brain dead." He threw a little flashlight against the tiled wall. "Who did this?"

The entire ER staff uttered a sob.

"Not sure who he is, but he's dead," said a state policeman, standing in the corner. "We're involved because Chief Strait shot him dead."

"Good! Give Chief a medal," Dr. Varner replied.

Stanley called Danielle at nine thirty. "I'll be home in a little bit, honey. This has been an awful one. I love you."

"I love you, too."

The warm, moist, foggy breeze blew Stanley's hair around as he walked through the sliding ER doors towards the employee parking lot. He pulled his fogged glasses off just before the crosswalk, wiping them on his sleeve, and smelled the musty air with a deep breath.

A black BMW idled with the headlights off. The bald driver

watched Stanley approach, just thirty feet away. He took his foot off the bake, put the car in gear and pushed the accelerator to the floor. The black car's rear wheels spun on the wet pavement and then the car lurched forward.

The sensation of his skull crunching through the BMW's windshield, the sound of all the colors, catapulting into the air, landing on the car's trunk, amazed Stanley's confused mind. He slid from the trunk, landing head first on the wet pavement. The black car sped away and turned left at the intersection. Steve Chase drove north on the Seven Hills Highway leading to the interstate and the Canadian border.

Nancy found Stanley first. Leaving the ER, she walked quickly towards the wet clump in the darkness, lying in the crosswalk. For a brief instant, her mind seemed unable to comprehend. She slumped to her knees in a bloody puddle. Stanley's arms were crumpled beneath his body. His face lay on its left cheek, blood oozing from his mouth and nose. Both eyes were partially open without blinking. He took slow, shallow breaths. Nancy felt a weak, rapid carotid pulse.

"Stanley…no…no…no…not you," she whispered, wiping the blood from the nose of the man who was her mentor and friend. She looked all around, searching for help, not wanting to leave him.

"GET A STRETCHER!" she screamed, spotting two third-shift nurses climbing out of their cars. "Hurry! It's Stanley."

The young ladies ran.

***

Machete put the cards down on the end of the poker table. "Stanley is hurt," he said.

The men around the table put their cards down too and stared at their blind friend.

"How?" Timothy asked from behind the bar.

"I just know he's hurt."

***

Danielle had a tall glass of Basil Hayden's on the rocks waiting on the table next to Stanley's favorite deck chair. She had the heaters burning and sipped a glass of Santa Chistina, expecting to hear her husband's Avanti roaring up the hill at any moment.

The sudden chill scared her, followed by a deep sadness she could not comprehend. She put the glass of wine down, pulling a blanket around her.

***

The phone behind the bar rang at Poor Joe's.

"Timothy, Jack here…Stanley has been hit by a car. Send someone to get Danielle."

"Jack?"

"I don't know. It's bad."

Timothy looked from behind the bar at the men gazing at him from the poker table. He uttered words he could not believe, "Stanley's bad hurt boys."

His mind flashed to the siege of the U.S. Embassy in Saigon.

…Wendell leaping high…catching a grenade thrown over the wall…the concussion knocking him against hot 50 cal.…Wendell crumpled in the mud, a tight curl, swearing…

He looked at Wendell sitting at the table.

Danielle listened to the front door opening and jumped a little. She had not heard the rumble from the Avanti. Carla walked through the French doors and stood still, crying, and Danielle knew.

"He's in the ER, Danielle."

"Why?"

"Timothy called me. I don't know. Tess is getting Charles out of the car; she'll stay here with the kids. Let's go."

"The last thing he said is 'I love you.'" Danielle put her hands to her cheeks. "He said, 'I love you. I'll be right home.'"

...hugging Stanley...Mallory Square growing distant in the mist...leaving Key West on Captain O'Malley's boat, headed for Cuba..."I love this life of adventure. You make me laugh, honey..."

***

The desperation in the Emergency Room did not affect the quiet determination to save their friend and mentor. Dr. McCaferty stood at the head of the stretcher, giving concise orders. Dr. Smith worked without saying a word while nurses handed him the equipment he needed without asking. The neurosurgeon, Dr. Varner, began his assessment. The on-call pulmonologist walked in just as Dr. Smith intubated Stanley, protecting his airway as the seizures began…just little ones at first.

"I'm sorry, honey. I love you very much."

Stanley tried to reach for Danielle from his darkness; nothing would move. The commotion around him seemed distant, fading further and further.

"I love you," came through the darkness again.

…Grandmother Rogers stood in the brightness. Janet Sue took his hand and walked towards her. Chief of Police Charles Johnson and Norma were waiting, too. They hugged. Then HE stood with them, just as he remembered HIM, smiling that same smile of love. "Not now." HE said with his arm around Stanley. "Not now. I need you to stay with them." HE waved as Stanley left, just like the first time…

The pain inside his head burned white. With lighting speed, Stanley grasped the intubation tube with what had been a limp right hand and ripped it from his throat. Coughing bloody froth, he thrashed about. Everything hurt everywhere.

Danielle threw her body over Stanley, holding each side of the stretcher, keeping her husband from falling. The nurses, Jillena, Nancy, and Crystal, each grabbed his legs and an arm, pinning them. Restraints were applied. Ramona held his left arm, with two IV's running, and she prayed for her good friend. Then Dr. Varner pushed a rapid acting IV sedative. Dr. Smith intubated his friend for the second time and squirted lidocaine down the tube.

"Get a CT stat!" Dr. Varner barked at no one in particular.

"Welcome back, my friend," Dr. McCaferty proclaimed with a hint of a smile.

Danielle looked up at him, and he nodded, *yes*.

Chapter Fifteen
Calling All Angels

Chief of Police Larry Strait secured the crime site quickly. Red and white sawhorses blocked both pedestrians and vehicles from crossing through the area. A nightshift patrolman had been stationed at the crosswalk for the entire night. At sunrise, Chief Strait and Timothy walked out of the hospital Emergency Room.

A state police investigation van pulled up to the Emergency Room entrance. The state troopers had driven all night from the state capital.

"This is no accident," Chief Strait said, pointing at black tire marks.

The state troopers measured the width of the rubber marks on the pavement and the distance from their beginning to the crosswalk. They took several pictures of the tread patterns.

Chief Strait stood from kneeling on the wet pavement, both knees wet with bloody rain water, his face red.

"It is a rear wheel drive; see how the tires slide from side to side before going forward...Some sort of traction control. The son-of-a-bitch sat waiting and then floored it. Manual transmission. There's where he shifted."

The troopers nodded in agreement while they measured and made notes on damp paper. They took more pictures of the pavement in the misty morning light.

"I'll fax these pictures to our IT guys," the shorter trooper said, water dripping from the bill of his hat. He walked towards the hospital. "We'll have a pretty good idea what we're dealing with in a little bit."

He returned seventeen minutes later.

"Yokohama tires, S drive. Given the car's width and manual transmission, the computer said high probably we're looking for a BMW 320i."

"I've got to go, Chief," Timothy said, shivering.

Larry Strait looked at Timothy's wet face.

Timothy shrugged and then muttered, "Make a call."

Chief Strait glanced at the troopers quickly. "Ok."

The taller of the troopers walked towards Chief Strait after Timothy left.

"Who's he calling?"

"His wife; we're close friends."

"Oh."

***

Stanley went directly from the CT scanner to the Operating Room. The CT showed a brain midline shift of 5 mm and a subdural hematoma 1 cm thick. Dr. Varner performed a Bur-Hole Craniostomy.

Sedated with a Propofol intravenous infusion and paralyzed with Zemuron, an endotracheal tube extended from his mouth while the ventilator made a gentle to and fro sound, Stanley slept. The operation went well. Doctor Varner evacuated the hematoma and there seemed to be no further bleeding.

Danielle sat on a blue chair pulled close to her husband's ICU bed. She played with the hair over his ear on the side that hadn't been shaved.

…it's not as long as when we met…getting a little gray at the temples…

She ran her fingers over the gray and twisted the curls around her forefinger.

...Ramona introduced me that day...right after moving from New Orleans...just an adventure...there you stood, behind the nurses' station...my new boss...your blue eyes staring...the first time we touched hands...lifting that old man off the ambulance stretcher into bed 2...when we were in the morgue together after the horrible accident and bloody night in the ER...with the cafeteria kids...we held hands in that cold morgue...the seductive way you hugged me when we sat on the warm cement at Mallory Square after dark...deciding to spend the rest of our lives together...I've loved you from that first stare, Stanley James McMillen...

***

Poor Joe's remained closed. The Usual Suspects lived in the ICU waiting room, even though they were not allowed into Stanley's room. Timothy and Carla had special dispensation and would give updates after talking with Danielle and looking at Stanley on the breathing machine.

The marque in front of the Big Bay Methodist Church simply stated, PRAYER MEETING FOR STANLEY SUNDAY 10 AM.

Timothy called Quinn O'Malley in Key West, Victor Bonifacio in St. Paul, and Rose Williams in Las Vegas. Then he called his old friends, musician David Chown in Traverse City, and singer Miriam Roosevelt in Carmel, California.

Friday, a Lear jet arrived from Key West. It had a little lion head painted on the fuselage. Saturday morning, identical jets arrived from St. Paul and then Las Vegas. Saturday afternoon Miriam and her husband arrived on a chartered jet, sent by Quinn O'Malley.

Pastor Katherine Kennedy McGinnis stood and looked out into the congregation. Her eyes filled with tears before she could utter a word.

"Today we are gathered together to pray for our dear friend. This is our Sunday service."

She looked through her blurry eyes at the front row, at Quinn O'Malley, Timothy, Carla, Miriam, Jim, Pete, Ralph, Wayne, Vincent, Rose, Jonathon, Doug with their son, and, in the second row, Richard Elmore Fortin, Chief of Police Strait and his wife Dawn, and Machete and Little Miss. They looked up at their red-haired Irish preacher, with questioning, almost pleading eyes, each soul in agony. The crowd filled the balconies on either side and spilled to the sidewalk through the big open front doors.

"He married us; Stanley married Doug and me. He married Miriam and Jim," she spoke, pointing towards the front row. "That is the kind of guy he is. Who knew that he has a PhD in Theology and is more knowledgeable than I am about religion—just his wife, and he wasn't too happy with her for sharing that...For as long as I have known him, it has been about other people how to help, how to heal, how to eliminate suffering in our bodies and in our souls, how to laugh one day at a time. Without trying, Stanley has shown us how to live this life without preventable regret, to forgive the unthinkable," she paused and glanced at Machete, "to never miss an opportunity to say I love you, to give a hug and always...always be ready to help friends, without regard to personal consequences."

Kate paused. Her chest beneath the robes heaved with sobs.

Timothy stood up from the front row. He turned towards the crowd. "He saved my life; Stanley saved my life when I was wounded in the cabin behind Benjamin's Seafood. I would not have survived that day if he hadn't been there in harm's way with the rest of us. He stopped the bleeding," he said, holding up the remains of his right arm, ending at the elbow.

"Stanley saved my husband's life." Chief Strait's wife stood up in the second row. "After Ric and Michelle's murder, Larry blamed himself for their deaths. He became so depressed. I came home and found him in our bedroom with his service pistol. All I could think was to call Stanley. He walked into our bedroom and lay down beside my husband and just started talking. Larry is here today; I have my husband because Stanley walked into a room with a man holding a gun and flopped on the bed beside him. I have never shared this until today."

Doug stood next.

"Well, he's saved me a bunch of times—clear back to the time I chased him down the hall on the third floor with a mop, and after my cardiac arrest; him and Dr. McCaferty have saved me, and I am thankful." He looked up at his red-haired wife, looking down at him from the podium.

Kate turned and nodded towards the choir loft. They sang:

"Calling all angels, calling all angels

Walk me through this one; don't leave me alone

Calling all angels, calling all angels

We're trying, we're hoping, but we're not sure how

OH. But if you could, do you think you would

Trade it all, all the pain and suffering?

Oh, but then you would've missed the beauty of

The light upon this earth and the sweetness of leaving

Calling all angels, calling all angels

Walk me through this one; don't leave me alone*. "

David Chown lifted his fingers from the pipe organ keys. There was no silence after the last chords from the pipe organ, but rather a sanctuary of sniffling, men coughing, and sobs.

"This is not a funeral," Kate said, regaining her composure, gazing at the multitude of friends and patients. "We are here to lift up our dear friend in prayer, to ask our Father in heaven to heal Stanley and have him stay with us a while longer.

"If it be your will, Father, please help Stanley; heal him. We need him. Thank you, Lord. Your will be done."

The sanctuary erupted in applause.

A young lady with long, blond hair and brilliant eyes squeezed into the last pew and sat next to an old man. He looked at her.

"You a patient of Stan's, too?" he asked.

"No, I'm just an old friend," she replied.

"Can't be for that long," he answered.

"You'd be surprised," she smiled back. And it was then that the old man realized she had not moved her lips, even once, and he worried he was coming down with Alzheimer's dementia.

From the pulpit, Kate spotted the young lady with brilliant eyes looking in her direction, and she knew.

Chapter Sixteen

Who are You Guys

They collided, she exiting from the first row pew walking in front of Timothy, and he, coming from the second row, not seeing her because of his blind right eye.

Richard turned face to face with Carla, staring at her.

...standing outside the tunnel leading from Poor Joe's and she running her fingers down the scar, my scar...what happened?...two fishermen, who had helped her open the heavy wooden door that wouldn't budge, walked back up the river into the mist with their mongrel dog following...her face looked up as she ran across the drug lord's compound with the True Believers...carrying a baby...and her face was covered with blood...for an instant, just an instant, she stopped and stared at me in the pilot's seat...Quinn O'Malley named it Operation Two Hearted...flew the True Believers as fast as I dared...twenty minutes...410 at fifty feet...just above the tree tops to rescue her...a big bird hit the navigator's windshield and cracked it...some of the blood had been wiped away when we landed outside El Paso, but not all...she stood there, looking through the cabin door...thank you...thank you...thank you...tears washed clean little tracks through the smeared blood on her cheeks...

Richard breathed deeply, feeling Carla's heart pounding in their embrace and smelling her faint perfume.

"Why are you here, Richard?" There was alarm in her voice. "You shouldn't be here."

"For Stanley; O'Malley flew me in last night. Leaving at 1400. It's great to see you again, Carla."

Timothy leaned in and shook Richard's hand. "Thanks for coming, friend."

Six men surround them.

"Time to go," one of them said.

Richard, with the men leading, pushed through the crowd at Big Bay Methodist Church and into a silver Mercedes S 500 with thick, glass windows.

***

Vincent Bonifacio sat at the head of the poker table with Timothy to his right. Quinn O'Malley sat at the other end with Chief Strait next to him. Rose and Carla sat across from each other; Carla was shaking next to her husband.

The Poor Joe's *OPEN* sign remained off well past the time it would have been switched on for lunch. At twelve fifteen, two state policemen walked through the front door and looked at Chief Strait.

"Who are these people and why are they at our meeting?" the shorter man in blue asked.

"It's my bar," Timothy shot back. "My bar...my friend...my party."

"You can drive up to the capital and meet us at the post, Chief; we're leaving," the older state policeman said.

"SIT DOWN," Vincent Bonifacio said, "and listen or I'll see you both reassigned to the mother of all ghettos."

They stopped and turned. The one with captain bars on his shirt collar raised his right arm toward Vincent, the forefinger pointing.

"I'd listen to him," Chief Strait said, "I don't think he's kidding."

Confusion flashed over the younger man's eyes, standing next to his captain.

Quinn O'Malley reached into a leather briefcase on the floor next to his chair and withdrew a manila folder that he tossed on the table.

"Have a seat, gentlemen; let's see what we have here."

The state policemen sat on either side of Rose.

"Captain Jonathon Miles, says here you've been with the state police fifteen years after serving your country with distinction as a United States Marine. Says you have a Purple Heart. Semper Fi."

He paused long enough to look at Jonathon, eye to eye.

"Says you are an inspector, Aaron Truman. Congratulations on your recent promotion, young man. Four years in army intelligence before you joined the State Police. Married with a son and another child on the way; congratulations, again."

The bar was silent except for the pop popping from the old popcorn machine in the corner next to the front door.

"All right, who are you guys?" State Police Captain Miles asked.

"Well, Captain." Timothy said, "This is Vincent Bonifacio. Owns an Italian import-export business in St Paul, Minnesota. And this is Rose Williams, owner of several casinos in Vegas, and at the end down there sits Captain Quinn O'Malley from Key West; has a one-boat charter business."

Captain Miles leaned back in his chair and took a deep breath. He looked at Quinn O'Malley and exhaled slowly before saying, "The True Believers."

"What?" the inspector uttered in confusion.

"Later," his captain said abruptly.

"We need your help. Need to work together on this," Timothy said. "The bastard is still at large."

"You're making several assumptions," Captain Miles said.

"My wife is here to share a conversation she had with Stanley's wife. To be honest, I'm concerned for Danielle's safety as well. Go ahead, honey."

Carla's complexion matched the color of the gray coffee mug in her trembling right hand. She looked at her husband through the side of her wide eyes.

...Raul Veracruz holding a big bolt cutter with red handles, a handle in each hand, making the blades open and close...his lieutenant pushing me and baby Charles closer and closer towards his desk...his head exploding, splattering the white wall behind him...pee running down my leg...Charles under me on the floor, screaming...

"Danielle had a boyfriend in high school, since eighth grade actually, and all through college. They were going to get married, but Danielle moved to Big Bay and he moved to Alaska. Danielle flew to Alaska to break off the engagement after she fell in love with Stanley. That was nine years ago."

She lifted the mug. It shook, spilling coffee over the lip.

"Danielle told me last week that this guy has been calling her for a month and hanging up after saying 'I love you.' She's so scared."

Rose spoke next.

"The scum bag's name is Steven Mark Chase. D.O.B. 7/15/55. Lives in Anchorage, Alaska. Educated as an engineer; graduated at the top of his class; has an IQ around 140; owns a company subcontracted to maintain the Trans-Alaska Pipeline. He invented something called a 'pig' that looks for corrosion inside the pipeline. Married for eight years, three children."

"The Canadian Mountie's say a BMW rental car passed through into Canada at the Niagara Falls gate. Records say the driver stated he had business in Labrador City and that he had hit a deer, when asked about the cracked windshield," Vincent Bonifacio interjected. "Steve Chase rented a black BMW at the Boston Airport."

"I'm not sure you guys need our help," Captain Miles said.

Quinn O'Malley smiled. "We're just business owners, Captain. If we come across information of interest, we'll share it with your office. The State Police can bring this case to justice."

"I understand," the captain replied. "Got it."

Carla slapped the table several times with her hands, left then right, over and over, splattering coffee.

"I WANT SOMEONE TO GUARD DANIELLE, LIKE MACHETE GUARDED ME, WHEN I CAME HOME FROM MEXICO BEFORE HE WAS SHOT!"

Every face turned towards her red face.

"I want Richard Fortin to guard her. I want you guys to keep him safe and get him back here. Call whomever the hell you need to call. No one will mess with Danielle while Richard watches her. I mean it, Timothy, Quinn, and you," she said, pointing at Captain Miles.

"We'll assign a guard," the inspector said.

"Richard will guard Danielle with his soul. Will your trooper do that?"

"Who is this Fortin?" asked the captain. He looked at O'Malley. "Oh, one of yours?"

"Yes, sir; one of the finest. You'd have been proud to serve with him."

"I'm sure that's true, General O'Malley."

***

"Who the hell are the True Believers?" asked Inspector Aaron Truman.

"You wouldn't believe it if I told you," replied Captain Jonathon Miles, driving the unmarked police car out of Poor Joe's parking lot. "And you were in Army Intelligence."

"Try me."

"Private special forces that fly in German engineered Stealth, radar invisible helicopters at 400 miles per hour."

"You're right."

"Told you."

"C.I.A. believes they had six built before the plans were destroyed."

"Where do they keep them?" Inspector Truman asked.

"Don't know. Rumors say Cuba and Mexico, maybe Canada. No one admits the True Believers exist."

"Well," the younger state policeman said, "we just saw them."

"Right, an import grocer, casino owner, and one-boat charter captain. Think anybody's going to believe you?"

"Good point."

Chapter Seventeen

This One I Love

Doctors McCaferty, Smith, Varner, and a pulmonologist stood next to Stanley's ICU bed across from Danielle, her head on a pillow next to her husband's right arm.

"No seizure activity for 72 hours on the EEG. I started titrating the drips off ninety minutes ago," Dr. Varner said.

"We should get him extubated soon or trach him," Dr. McCaferty commented.

"He's breathing on his own; vent's just on standby since ten this morning," the pulmonologist added. "O2 sat running around 97 percent."

"Let's skip the noon conference and meet back here," Dr. Smith said. He grinned.

"Special dispensation from Chief of Staff."

***

"Danielle, why don't you wait outside while we get Stan extubated," Dr. Smith said, leaning close with his hand on her back.

"No," she answered.

"You don't need to see this; I'll come get you."

"I've helped extubate hundreds of patients, Lavern. This one I love;

why wouldn't I want to help now?"

Danielle stood, pushing her chair to the wall. She turned the wall suction on high, looking at the physicians, yankaur suction in her hand.

"Here's what you guys can't do," she said. With her lips touching his right ear, Danielle spoke, "I love you very much, honey. We're going to get this damn tube out now, so you can say it too. OK?"

The pulmonologist deflated the bulb at the endotube. Danielle placed the yankaur suction tip in her husband's mouth. Stanley coughed bloody mucous while Danielle suctioned, all the while quietly repeating several times, "You're ok, honey, you're ok. I love you."

Then the only sound in the room came from the whistling yankaur suction. Seven ICU nurses stood at the entrance to room 3, watching. The physicians nervously watched the blood pressure waveforms undulating up and down. Dr. McCaferty's eyes stared at the cardiac monitor.

Dr. Varner watched the oxygen monitor and felt Stanley's radial pulse.

Danielle put her face close to her husband's, nose to nose, breathing his breath, breathing in unison in and out, sharing life, soul to soul, talking quietly, telling him she adored him.

Stanley's wide eyes looked at the contraptions in the room and then moved from face to face then back to Danielle's face.

"Love you," he said with a hoarse voice. "Let's go home."

The nurses in the doorway clapped.

Richard Elmore Fortin smiled a crooked smile as he peeked between two of the nurses. He listened to the sounds coming from the other ICU rooms: the ventilators making gentle breathing sounds, little warning beeps and alarms. He closed his eye and inhaled the seaweed odors of betadine and the smell of rubbing alcohol. The patient in the next room moaned a young girl's moan.

…white hot burning from deep inside the right leg…impossible to hurt like this…the nurse squeezing my hand and injecting morphine into

the IV...I see the color of it and taste it too. Marie hugging me tight around my neck, kissing my cheeks over and over...the doctors discussing taking me to the operating room...Quinn O'Malley...in the seat behind me, the biplane trainer...flying over Old Key West at 1000 feet..."she's all yours," O'Malley's voice to me...guts cramping..."she's all yours" crackled in the head set..."my hands are in the air"...either you fly us back or we meet your baby sister...

"You're not allowed in here, mister," the young man's voice said from behind.

Richard looked over his left shoulder and followed the young security guard moving to face him. The young man took several little steps backwards when he saw the right eye and the scar—the right eye staring, not blinking. Richard opened his brown jacket, revealing a large gold badge affixed to a thin bulletproof vest.

"I am here at the request of State Police Commissioner Rollins to provide protection for the McMillen's. I would appreciate any help you can afford."

"Yes, sir!" the young man replied, straightening from his slouch.

"Hi, Richard," a hoarse voice said from the bed. "Come meet my wife."

"That was a close one, Jack," Dr. Varner said as he and Dr. McCaferty walked towards the noon conference downstairs.

Chapter Eighteen

A Flying Lamborghini

The Steersman two-seater biplane lifted quickly from the Key West runway. The 7-cylinder radial piston engine pounded, vibrating like the John Deere pulling a 3-bottom plow. Richard smiled. Quinn O'Malley flew the old plane directly to Cuba, only once speaking on the radio in Spanish as they entered Cuban territory. They circled Havana and headed north, flying over Fort Jefferson on the Dry Tortugas.

"I speak Spanish," Richard said while they circled Havana.

"I know; it was your minor at the Academy. It's going to be useful."

They flew over Key West at 1000 feet, circling twice.

"Got your bearings?" O'Malley asked.

"Yes, sir, that's Mallory Square. The airport is directly ahead."

"My hands are in the air, Captain Fortin; she's all yours."

Burning, intense abdominal cramping, Richard felt the warm sensation of his pants filling with liquid feces.

...rolling over and over again and again...the sun blinding and then gone and then back, over and over...poor broken machine groaning..."you can do it, big brother...you can do it," Marie cheering...her brown eyes sparkling..."you can do it, big brother...you

can"...

A burst of gulf air rising from the island lifted the biplane. It pitched to the right and slowly spiraled towards the ground.

"She's all yours, Group Captain."

The plane continued to spiral downward, the old engine whining a high pitch, the bi-wings groaning.

"Or, we can meet your baby sister right now," cracked in the headphones.

Richard put his feet and hands on the controls. He tipped the plane directly at the ground. With the wings screeching and the patrons at Schooner Wharf Bar coming closer by the second, he pulled back and lifted the plane out of the dive, 200 feet from the ground.

...see...told you...big brother...

"That may get us an FAA warning. We'll just say we had engine problems." Captain O'Malley chuckled in the headphones.

"When were you going to get us out of that spin?" Richard asked, climbing down from the cockpit.

"I wasn't kidding, Richard."

Going from the hanger towards the parking lot, Captain O'Malley put his arm on Richard's shoulder.

"I saw her up there with you; she's cute."

"What color is her hair?"

"Reddish brown, curly. She has brown eyes."

"Yup, you read that someplace?"

"Nope. And I sure as hell hoped you'd listen to her."

"You did, huh?"

"Tomorrow we're going to take a little boat ride to Havana."

"Why?"

"I have a friend who needs your help. And, you're gonna love his helicopter." He paused and stopped. "Man, you stink."

***

The tall man with a short, black beard stood up from behind a desk when Richard and Quinn entered the room.

He puffed twice on a cigar.

"You are smaller than I thought," Fidel Castro said in Spanish.

Richard stared back into the brown eyes that seemed to be recording everything.

"Just don't climb into the ring with this little man, my friend," Quinn said with a laugh.

"The champion from your state of Ohio learned that too late," Fidel replied, finally smiling. He extended his right hand to Richard.

"Welcome to Havana."

Fidel Castro trimmed the ends of three cigars.

"Eduardo Ribera makes these for me," he said, handing Quinn and Richard a cigar.

"Cohiba." He smiled. "Delicious."

"My friend here tells me that you're perhaps the best helicopter pilot in the U.S. Air Force."

Richard stepped back, looking at Fidel Castro and Quinn O'Malley standing next to each other, Castro three inches taller.

"How long have you known each other?" he asked in their direction.

"We have been friends since law school, University of Havana. We have known each other many years now. O'Malley saved my life in the early years of the rebellion. I trust him with my life."

Richard exhaled a deep breath, his cheeks puffed out.

"I love flying helicopters. I feel their heart beating. I do the thinking; the machine protects me, and I keep it safe."

Fidel's brown eyes did not blink a single time, watching Richard speaking.

"You were shot down in Honduras," Fidel said.

Richard stared intently at Fidel and stepped closer, looking up.

"The evil ones shot my Marie. The day will come when I find them, the ones who hurt Marie, and I will kill them."

"I know who did it," Castro replied. "I like your answer. We have the same enemy."

Richard looked at Quinn.

"Drug cartel in Honduras, Richard."

"I hate the drug cartels," Fidel said emphatically. "I hate them. They ruin our young ones. And they hate me. They have sold their souls to Satan for a profit. Will you join me, Quinn O'Malley's friend?"

Richard Elmore Fortin extended his hand towards Fidel Castro.

"I am honored, Mr. President."

Fidel looked at Quinn and raised his eyebrows.

"Should we show Richard our machine?"

***

They flew in a green Mi-8 Russian helicopter to the heavily guarded San Antonio de Banus Airfield, 30 miles southwest of Havana.

With the face of poker players holding a winning hand, they watched Richard's expressions while the huge armored garage door ratcheted into the ceiling, revealing their pride.

Richard left them, walking as though hypnotized, towards the black flying machine. He walked along its entire length, his right hand feeling the smoothness of the composite construction, rubbing the short wings extending from the fuselage concealing jet engines. At the tail he looked back, marveling.

"She's a flying Lamborghini!" Richard said, with the enthusiasm first felt when his father purchased a new John Deere. "I just love her. Let's go for a ride!"

"It flies a bit difficult, Group Captain…takes three up front."

"Well, we got three," Richard said, still excited.

"I just ride, and don't trust O'Malley to fly anything that goes over one hundred," Fidel said while waving towards two men dressed in black.

For 30 minutes the navigator and co-pilot, tucked into the seats next to Richard, discussed flying controls in Spanish and how the thrusters worked. Richard grinned the entire time. The charter boat captain and president of Cuba sat in the back, listening to the conversations in the cockpit, smiling together.

Flying at 2000 feet over Cuba at 350 miles per hour, Richard closed his eyes and listened to the soul of this machine throb rhythmically.

...faster...faster...faster, Marie shouted, straddling the hand-hewn wooden beam that extended the entire length of the barn...see...told you...faster, Richard...

Richard pushed the throttle forward. The Stealth helicopter lurched ahead, reaching 400 miles per hour.

Fidel Castro shook Quinn O'Malley's hand.

Chapter Nineteen

God's Still Mad

Judith Newman sat in the comfortable chair next to her pastor's desk, the chair now pulled close to Kate. Through the window, Kate glanced to see the red and yellow leaves dancing, circling towards the cold ground.

Five weeks previous, Judith, from her front door, had watched dreams transforming into a horrendously incomprehensible slow-motion murder. Tiffany's screaming gurgles replayed without distraction, Judith's mind racing through the event over and over without resting.

Judith's broken-hearted soul stared at Katie.

"I need help," she said after several minutes of silence but for the tick ticking of the Old Ben desk clock.

"I don't know what to do."

"I'll help, Judy. Talk to me."

"Two years ago this March, I lost Mike. I found him on the Allis-Chalmers, slumped on the fender, all cold. He loved that old tractor. I lost the love of my heart. I dream about him almost every night."

She paused to blow her nose. Looking at the floor now, twisting the wet Kleenex into a rope, she tore little pieces from the end, watching them drop to the floor.

"Then Tiffany and the children came to live with me." She looked up into Kate's eyes with complete agony. "I was relieved that they were home, away from him, and I could help my only child put the pieces of her life back together."

Judith Newman looked desperately at her pastor. "Where was God when we needed help? Why didn't He help, strike that evil man down? I kept screaming to God to help us. Tiffany cried out to Jesus, one time. Blood was all over the lawn, Katie. My husband and now my beautiful Tiffany...I can't do this anymore."

"I don't know, Judy. I don't know the reason evil is allowed. I hate it. It's the first question I'll have when I meet God. Why the evil, when we didn't need it? We could have made choices without evil. I don't know. Breaks my heart, too."

Kate reached for Judith's right hand and held it tight.

"God saw his son murdered a horrible death. All I know, Judy, is that, if I was God, you and I would not be having this conversation, because I would have destroyed all humanity at that moment, would have just said to my son, 'Come on home, they aren't worth it.'" She paused. "I would have left the dogs in charge, the dogs and dolphins, I think...and the Bonobo apes. That's how much He loves us. He loves us like a dog loves us, no conditions, just love."

"I think God's still mad at us."

"I don't think love knows revenge, Judy. But I confess, what confuses me is why the pain and suffering while we make our choices, why the barbarians are allowed to exist? I truly am going to ask that question first, right after I hug Jesus. My heart ached after Ric and Michelle were murdered, when Stanley was almost killed, and when Tiffany was taken on the same day."

Kate watched Judith who was looking down, dropping little bits of twisted tissue paper, which mixed with the tears on the hardwood floor.

Judith breathed a deep sigh.

"I just can't do it anymore, Kate. I know it's only been a little while. I'm all done in. Every morning I wake up and wish I hadn't, that I was waking up in heaven with Mike and Tiffany. When I change little Jamie's diaper, I see little Tiffany and I start crying. Then Joey and Beth start crying and don't want to get on the school bus. I want to die, Kate. I want to be with my husband and my daughter."

She stopped and looked at the sleeping baby in the car seat leaned against the office wall.

"But, there's no one to take care of Tiffany's…" She shook her head back and forth. "The son-of-a-bitch's family out in La Jolla will have nothing to do with our family. I'm all they got, and I'm all done in. Some days I think I should turn the gas on when we go to bed so we can all go home together."

"Judy, I'm going to get you some help," Kate said. She picked up the phone.

Dr. Rink cancelled her office appointments for the afternoon. She pulled a chair towards Judith in Kate's office and listened to the sorrow pour out. She listened to the desperation and the gloomy agony.

"I want you to come with me, Judy, right now," Dr. Rink said, lifting the sleeping five-month-old girl from the car seat and handing her to Kate. "We're going to the hospital. Kate and Doug will take care of the children," she said, looking directly at Kate. "They will love the children. We will get you help."

Judith looked at Kate, uncertainty in her wide, blue eyes. She held her hand out, touching the baby.

"Would you and Doug adopt them, please? I think Jesus would like that."

Kate sat in her office chair, rocking back and forth, holding Tiffany's 5 month old daughter, who looked back at the pastor with her mother's and grandmother's blue eyes. Kate hummed and rocked for twenty minutes, thinking and praying.

Then she called her husband.

"Doug, what do you think about adopting Tiffany's children?"

She listened to him breathe in the receiver.

"I would love it."

"It's beyond our comprehension what these little souls have experienced, so lost with the memories of their dead daddy and murdered mom. I'll remember forever the two oldest sitting on either side of their grandmother at the funeral. When they got up from the front row and touched their mom's casket as it passed…ripped a hole in me, honey."

"We'll help them; Katie, we know love and we know loss, and we will love them with all our hearts," the old war vet said.

Kate could hardly hear him; he was talking that softly.

"I'll call Faith Lisenmayer. She was a big help when we adopted Danny."

" Yeah, Judge Lisenmayer and Richard Fortin!" Doug chuckled.

"Doubt we need Richard's help this time, Doug."

Chapter Twenty

Not a Single Thing to Fear

"**W**e think you should take three months off."

The words felt like the time when he was seven and he pushed his inquiring forefinger into the empty light socket. Over and over, a quivering shock traveled through his mind and down his extremities. He looked at Danielle and shrugged.

Doctors McCaferty, Smith, Fox, and Varner sat on their condo deck.

"It'll be a vacation, honey. We'll have fun and recharge our batteries."

Stanley leaned back in his favorite white wicker deck chair. He went from face to face with his eyes, looking into their eyes, while he rubbed the itchy side of his head where the hair had now grown to stubble length.

"I need to do a comb over." He smiled, itching at the bur-hole scar. "When am I allowed to have a little Basil's again?"

"Another week, Stan, after the next neuro check. I think another week," Dr. Varner said.

"Ok if we take a trip after the checkup, say to Cuba?"

Danielle looked quickly from physician to physician, fear leaking from her hazel eyes.

"No leaving the country, Stan. No flying for the foreseeable future," Dr. Smith replied.

"Well, shit!"

From the chair just inside the open French doors came, "I have a home in Key West. I will drive you there."

They all turned their heads. Richard Elmore Fortin stood from his guarding position in the living room and walked through the French doors.

"There's plenty of room—three bedrooms, and a swimming pool," he said.

"Am I allowed to swim?" Stanley asked with a little sarcasm. "I'm sorry. I'm sorry, guys."

"You can leave after next week's evaluation," Dr. Varner said.

Danielle helped her husband stand.

He walked from doctor to doctor, stopping and shaking each man's hand.

"Thank you…Thank you…Thank you…Thank you," he repeated.

When he reached the doorway, he turned, and, with Danielle's arm supporting him, continued, "Thank you for saving my life. Thank you for saving my daughter's life. Where we are headed is much brighter than here. The light makes beautiful music. Chief Johnson and Norma said to tell you guys hi. There's not a single thing to fear, guys, but thank you."

His friends stared at their friend and smiled.

Danielle squeezed him.

"He's right," Richard said.

***

"I like Key West in the winter!" Stanley said to the friends packed into Poor Joe's for the going away party. Stanley raised a small glass of Basil Hayden's on the rocks.

"This is my first Basil's." He grinned and drank the entire small glass. "One more; that is a pitiful little glass, Timothy; you should be ashamed."

Dr. Varner nodded approval to Timothy, who emptied the ice and filled the glass with amber deliciousness.

"A toast!" Dr. McCaferty said, raising his glass of Jamison 18 year old. "A toast to our friend, who visited the bright side. Stanley visited the great unknown and came back. May he live a long and happy life!"

"TO DADDY!" shouted nine-year-old Chloe Norma, holding a glass of RC Cola high.

"It is bright there, Doctor McCaferty!"

She sure looks like Danielle, Stanley thought. He leaned close to his wife. "You know, we need to get Chloe enrolled in the Key West school."

"Already taken care of, honey. I sure am in love with you."

...and there she was, standing in the new CCU beside the director of nursing who was pissed because this new nurse had been hired by the administrator as a favor to his friend in

New Orleans. This was the most beautiful lady he had ever seen...

"For he's a jolly good fellow," said David Chown and he pounded on the keyboard of the old upright. Pete put his hands around Miriam Roosevelt's waist, lifting her to the piano top.

Sitting atop the upright, she led the crowd,

"FOR HE'S A JOLLY GOOD FELLOW. FOR STANLEY IS A JOLLY GOOD FELLOW..."

Richard Elmore Fortin sat on the stairs, halfway up, watching the crowd with his good eye.

Machete sat on the stairway landing, Little Miss beside him, watching too.

Chapter Twenty-One

An American Passport

The bald man walked into the Quonset hut next to the Yarmouth Airport terminal and extended his hand towards the man sitting behind a desk covered by stacks of papers.

"Need to hire a charter to Marathon, Florida. You have a plane that will do the job?"

The retired Royal Canadian Air Force pilot scratched his right ear.

"That's quite a flight there, fella; not cheap, either. What's your name?"

"P. Collin Morgan," Steve Chase said.

"Well, P. Collin Morgan, how'd ya get to Nova Scotia in the first place?"

"Flew into Amherst three days ago. Conducted some business with a Lobster Cooperative. Have a restaurant in New York, The Lobster Pot; maybe you've heard of it? Famous for seafood... Now I've got to get to Marathon ASAP to keep a deal together. Contract for flash frozen sea bass and grouper...today, tomorrow, at the latest."

"Nope, never heard of it."

He looked at a calendar with notes scribbled on various dates.

"The only time I can fly you, is this afternoon. I need to be back Wednesday. Let's see your passport."

"No passport. Here's my enhanced driver's license."

"I prefer a passport."

"Oh, wait," Steve said. He reached into his briefcase and then pushed a stack of one hundred dollar bills held together with a rubber band through the papers towards the man.

"It's an American passport."

The man looked at the bundle for several seconds, and then up at Steve.

"That's a proper document. Let's see that driver's license again."

He filled out a manifesto and flight plan.

"We leave at noon, precisely. Five hour trip, if we don't hit any weather. We'll make it without refueling in the King Air. That will be two thousand U.S. dollars, Mr. P. Collins

Morgan."

"You're kidding."

"I certainly am not," the man behind the desk, said, picking up the passport money.

***

"The Royal Canadian Police found a BMW with a VIN number, matching the missing car, from the Boston rental place," Quinn said on the phone to State Police Captain Jonathon Miles.

"Where?"

"Peggy's Cove."

"Don't know where that is, Quinn."

"Nova Scotia. Found the car sunk at the end of a boat ramp in ten feet of water. No plates. Lobster boat hit it this morning."

"And that Chase fellow, he inside?"

"We wouldn't be that fortunate, Jonathon."

"I'll call the Regional Police Headquarters in Halifax and fax them all the info we have."

"Thanks."

***

The phone rang at 817 White Street, twenty minutes after breakfast. Richard heard it ring from the front porch as he watched cars on the other side of the white picket fence go by, east and west.

Stanley heard it ring from his chair next to the pool while reading *The Key West Citizen* newspaper.

Danielle jerked a little when it rang. She put two coffee cups into the dishwasher and walked to the dining room.

"Hello?"

"I love you."

Chapter Twenty-Two

817 White Street

It slowed, approaching 817 White Street from the west, pulling over into the oncoming lane; then the car stopped, briefly. The rear driver's side window rolled down. A man with a

Detroit Tigers baseball cap pulled down over his eyes extended his arm, forming a pistol-pointing finger with his left hand.

Richard lifted the Luger from his lap and waved it at the car.

Then the blue Dodge squealed away.

Richard pulled a triangular-shaped phone from his pocket and called Quinn.

"He's here, Quinn."

"How do you know that?"

"He called this morning with his 'I love you' message. Drove by just now, stopped long enough to poke his arm out the window and make a pistol with his hand."

"Damn, he's a nut, Richard," Quinn said.

"And he's got help," Richard continued. "He was in the back seat."

"Keep Danielle and Stanley in the house and lock the doors. I'll send help while we figure a secure location. I'm going to the grade school and pick up Chloe."

"The school gonna let you?"

"Yup, I'm Uncle Quinn."

***

Danielle helped Stanley out of the recliner next to the pool surrounded by a tall white wooden fence.

"I'm still dizzy when I stand."

"I know, honey."

"Why?"

"Why what?'

"Why do I have to go in?"

From deep inside Danielle began to tremble. She felt the tears forming and felt like peeing.

"Richard! Come help!"

"No, stay out there," Richard replied, carrying a 12 gauge shotgun in his left arm and a Luger pistol in his right hand. "I think we are safer out here."

He stopped, looking through the open French doors at Danielle hugging her husband, their bodies fused, trembling as one. Stanley's eyes looked bewildered.

"We need to tell him," Richard said.

They sat around the picnic table under the big yellow umbrella. Richard sat so he could see both the fence gate and the back door.

"It's my old boyfriend that hit you with his car outside the ER, honey."

"Now that man carries a grudge; it's been ten years since we had that fight in Poor Joe's."

"I'm glad you never talked about it. Carla told me. It's worse than that."

"He's been calling me for the past two months, telling me that he loves me. He called here after breakfast. HE CALLED ME HERE...I'm so scared. CHLOE...CHLOE'S AT SCHOOL!"

"Quinn's picking her up," Richard said. "And he's sending help here."

A tiger cat climbed a Christmas palm tree and jumped over the fence. Richard twisted the Luger pistol aimed, and then put the gun back on the table.

The strange shaped phone rang in Richard's right pocket.

"Quinn has Chloe. On his way here."

"Whew," Danielle whispered.

"Why'd he hit me? All I did was knock him out during a fight he picked."

"He's a damn sicko, Stan—a twisted mind at work. We'll find him," Richard said, staring at the fence door with his good eye.

***

"Two things need to happen right now," Quinn O'Malley said to the group sitting at the dining room table. 817 White Street was surrounded by four uniformed Key West policemen and six men wearing bulletproof vests under their Caribbean Soul shirts, except for the two at the front door wearing Tommy Bahama shirts. The men in festive shirts each had a small tattoo on the inside of their right forearms: a small black lion.

"We need to get Stanley and his family to a secure location. I've made a phone call and should have a plan soon."

He paused as the Key West chief of police walked through the front door, holding a manila folder in his hand.

"And we need to secure the island. We have the bastard trapped on a piece of land three by five miles where everybody knows everybody, just one bridge off, one airport, and marinas easily patrolled."

The chief of police opened the folder and handed Quinn two glossy black and white photos.

"Pictures captured on Fausto's Grocery security camera. Shows the two guys in the front seat pretty good."

Quinn O'Malley let out an involuntary sigh and then clenched his jaw. Those at the table watched his eyes glisten with anger.

"Ramone Diaz and Raul Rodriguez, cousins to the recently departed Jesus Veracruz and bosses in the Mexican drug cartel."

Richard sat down, leaning the twelve-gauge against the wall. He rubbed under his glass eye and felt the scar on his forehead above the glass eye with his forefinger. For an instant his belly cramped. He rubbed his right leg.

...brilliant white flash and concussive force slamming above his eye...rat-a-tat-tat automatic gun sounds growing distant...

***

Fidel Castro had been furious. Twenty months ago, two men, a trusted friend, Major General Arnaldo Ochoa, and Cuba's Ministry of the Interior, had been caught and convicted of corruption. During their trials, they both revealed their contacts in the drug cartel and the routes used for the cocaine and heroin coming to Cuba.

The Mexican drug cartel was using Honduras as a distribution center for the Caribbean.

After an all-night meeting between Castro, his military advisors and Quinn O'Malley, twelve Cuban Special Forces and twelve men from the True Believers flew to an area west of Olanchito, Honduras, in two X-S 1 Stealth helicopters. Richard flew the lead machine. They landed and set up a command post in the jungle next to the Carr Saba Highway where it crossed the Rio Aguán River.

At 2 a.m., when the light from the harvest moon had been covered by fog, a cartel battalion attacked the Cuban Special Forces encampment. Three hundred cartel soldiers, armed with automatic weapons, grenade launchers, and a 50 cal. heavy machine gun attacked twenty-four Special

Forces soldiers and their six pilots.

Within 30 seconds, a distress signal was sent to Havana.

Richard's helicopter took a direct hit from a rocket-propelled grenade. Richard laid next to his broken machine, unconscious, blood oozing from his forehead and right eye.

***

They are Special Forces soldiers because they are special men.

***

Outnumbered 13 to 1, the True Believers and Cuban Special Forces repelled attack after attack, at times standing up from behind the large rocks and fallen trees, yelling at their attackers in the dark, chiding them, asking if they had their mommies with them. Three of the True Believers crawled through the jungle underbrush until they reached the 50 cal. machine gun. They shot the two Mexicans operating the machine gun with silencer-equipped pistols and dragged the big gun back.

"Now we have your machine gun," one of the True Believers shouted. They sent a salvo into the jungle, towards the attackers.

"Go tell your mommy we stole your machine gun."

It took 44 minutes from the start of the attack for the Cuban Air force to arrive. Fidel Castro had called the President of Honduras, advising him of the situation and not to interfere.

Hell-fire rained down from the MiG-21's. Twelve planes fired rockets as directed by the Special Forces, then dropped napalm bombs, lighting the area next to the river as bright as daytime.

The jets circled, occasionally firing their guns into the jungle, while a Russian-built Heavy Transport helicopter landed next to the broken Stealth machine. Quinn O'Malley jumped out. He carried an unconscious Richard to the waiting Heavy Transport. Two Cuban Special Forces had been wounded and were assisted aboard.

The Heavy Transport then lifted slowly. Straps tightened, and very slowly, the broken Stealth helicopter left the ground dangling beneath the Transport. The machines flew west, the broken machine and its unconscious pilot.

Two cartel ground lieutenants watched from the jungle as the machines flew away. Ramone Diaz and Raul Rodriguez watched with disgust. "Next time," one cousin said to the other.

...the foggy darkness became illuminated by the sounds of many colors. He and Marie were the same size. Her hug felt like a warm bath, and their hearts pounded as one...

"I'm sorry." The voice of Quinn O'Malley drifted through the bandages and confusion.

"You're in the hospital, Richard."

A screwdriver penetrated his right eye, being twisted around and around and around.

"This hurts more than the Blackhawk crash, Quinn."

"Your face will never be as pretty again, either."

"Thanks."

"Who attacked us?"

"Mexican cartel. An informer says the battalion is commanded by two cousins from the Mexico City Veracruz family. It was a setup, Richard. They were waiting."

***

Quinn handed the glossy photos to Richard.

"It's the cartel cousins for sure," Quinn said.

"What are they doing with Steve Chase?" Richard asked.

"Pretty brazen, even for them," The police chief said, taking the pictures from Richard.

"Not really, Chief...unfortunately," O'Malley replied.

Danielle stood in the kitchen listening, squeezing tight her nine-year-old daughter.

Chloe looked very much like her mother.

Chapter Twenty-Three

Can't Get any Crazier

Doug and Wendell sat at the little table in the southwest corner, with Machete and Little Miss.

Pete, Wayne, and Ralph the barber, sat around the long poker table in Poor Joe's. Dr. McCaferty had just joined them after a long day in the office, when Timothy stepped out from the red phone booth imported from London after World War One.

"Just when we think it can't get any crazier," he said. He leaned over the bar and drew a draft Schlitz.

The men glanced at each other. Timothy never drank alcohol while working.

"O'Malley just told me that that Steve Chase has followed Danielle and Stanley to Key West."

He took a long suck from the beer mug.

"And that's not the half of it; he's in the company of two notorious cartel bosses, cousins of our very own Jesus Veracruz," he said, pointing towards the dark blood stain near the front entrance.

"Holy shit!" exclaimed Wendell.

"Quinn said they have the house protected. He's confident Chase will not do anything like blowing the place up with Danielle inside. The real problem is they can't let Stanley go any place for fear of a sniper."

"We should go," Pete said, "and help our friends; we should go guys…"

"We all stay right here," Machete said. "The cartel knows where Big Bay is, too. You guys need to stay right here, out of O'Malley's way. I'll bet he has his Special Forces guys all over the island. And besides, he's got that crazy Richard Elmore Fortin, the only man without fear I have ever met."

"Why's that?" Timothy asked as he leaned over the bar for another draft.

"He has met with God. Richard does not fear danger, my amigos; he has no fear of dying again."

The bar became silent, except for Little Miss' tail thumping on the hardwood floor next to Machete.

"You see more than you let on," Dr. McCaferty said.

"I have stared down my demons, Doctor, and I have been forgiven for a past I cannot comprehend. I see clearly the colors of love, and I can see the blackness of evil. I'm not afraid of either. Trust me. We should all stay right here and protect Big Bay," the little Mexican said, staring at Dr. McCaferty with eyes blinded since that gunshot to his head.

Even the sound of Little Miss' tail stopped. She licked Machete's hand.

The phone rang in the phone booth. Timothy jumped off the bar stool and ran down the hallway.

"Fidel just called back," Quinn O'Malley said. "He insists that Stanley and his family be flown to his villa in Nueva Gerona on the Isle of Youth. He has already discussed it with our president and is sending an XS-1 to the Key West Airport at 2100 hours."

"That place is a fort, Quinn. They'll be safe there."

"For sure, Timothy; we'll keep you informed on our hunt."

Click.

Timothy walked down the hallway with every eye watching.

"Fidel Castro is sending one of those Stealth helicopters from

Havana at 9 p.m. to pick up Stanley and Danielle and fly them to his villa on the Isle of Youth."

"Wow!" exclaimed Pete and Wayne. They had been at the villa during negotiations with the cartel godfather, nine years ago.

"They'll be safe," Machete said with a smile, remembering that very trip and the beauty of it. "They will be very safe there."

"Richard used to fly those Stealth helicopters for the True Believers before he lost his eye," Machete continued.

"How'd you know that?" asked Pete.

"He told me and Little Miss one day. We talked one afternoon in my room. He misses his sister. I told him about my sister..." He stroked Little Miss' head, "...and that she came back."

...the yellow light from the lone ghetto street lamp still working outside, beamed through the holes instantly with the bang...bang...rat-a-tat...boom...boom...from handguns and automatic rifles, then a shotgun...the tar-paper wall shredded and baby sister Maria's crib...red dripping on mother's body lying next to the crib on the floor...

The men looked at their blind little Mexican friend.

Machete looked up from Little Miss.

"Yup, she came back to me."

Chapter Twenty-Four

One Naked Picture

Her children had left for school. Belvia Chase looked in the bathroom mirror at her reddened eyes and pulled her shoulder length soft brown hair into a ponytail.

Two Alaska State Police vehicles, both white Ford Explorers, hoods painted black, drove east on Coastal Trail, followed by a black GMC Suburban with blue lights hidden in the grill. All three vehicles turned right when they reached 2nd Avenue and pulled into the driveway leading to the large brown house.

KNOCK…KNOCK…KNOCK…hard against the front door. Belvia stiffened all over, afraid. She opened the front door, peering out at four men in uniform and one female dressed in a black suit.

"Have you found Steve?" she asked.

"No, Mrs. Chase, we are still looking. It would be helpful for purposes of this investigation to search your house," the lady officer in the black suit said.

"I don't know…"

"My name is Debra Williams; I'm with the D.E.A., Anchorage office. We have a search warrant. I'm sorry, this is important."

She handed a paper to Belvia.

"Why?"

"We're truly sorry for the inconvenience," Williams replied. "We shouldn't be long."

She walked to the door leading from the mudroom to the garage, turned and came back towards Belvia.

"I am truly sorry, Belvia. This must be heartbreaking and embarrassing. I'm sorry we are adding to your burdens," Agent Williams said.

"You know something, don't you?" Belvia said.

"Cloudy picture right now," Debra answered." Here's my card. Please call me anytime." She wrote her cell phone number on the back of the white card. "And, I will call you when we know more."

Ten minutes elapsed before one of the uniformed officers walked into the living room. Belvia looked up at the man holding a small red toolbox with a combination lock.

"You wouldn't happen to know the combination to this, would you?" he asked

"I've never seen it before."

"We'll need to cut the lock off, then."

"Whatever."

The officer walked back into the garage through the open mudroom door. Belvia watched as one man held the metal box on the wooden work counter, while a second officer snapped the lock off with a large bolt cutter.

She watched the officer open the red box, remove some pictures, and hand them to Agent Williams.

"Do you know who this is"?

Belvia took the pictures from Debra. She gasped and looked at Agent Williams with consternation when she came to the naked picture of Danielle standing on the beach.

"They look like high school pictures, Mrs. Chase…old high school pictures"

"I KNOW…WHY DOES HE STILL HAVE THEM! AND

LOCKED UP?" she shouted, trembling.

"Do you know why he would have a key labeled Merrill Field Airport?"

"He has a warehouse in the airport industrial park. Don't know why he'd have a key in that box. A naked girl…damn him!"

***

A swat team, led by Agent Williams, broke open the front door of the Chase Incorporated Warehouse, just as the short Alaska day faded towards darkness. For three hours they searched through the industrial equipment supplies, file cabinets, and barrels of chemicals labeled with skulls and crossbones.

"This key has to open something here," Agent Williams said, walking in a large circle, holding the key from the red box. She stopped and stared at a yellow High-Low tractor facing the north wall, parked with large shipping boxes on either side and one box on the lift. She walked outside with a flashlight, returning with a smile.

"There's a room on the other side of that wall, buried. Found a ventilation pipe poking out of the ground." She climbed on the High-Low, started it as the men watched, and backed it to the middle of the warehouse, revealing a gray, windowless metal door.

"Any of you guys want to bet on whether this key unlocks that door?"

She trotted to the gray door and unlocked it.

The small room contained bales of marijuana stacked from the floor, touching the 12-foot ceiling.

On the west wall stood a row of gray filing cabinets with large metal drawers. Each drawer contained multiple bags filled with white powder.

"Well, now we know why Mr. Steve Chase was in the company of Ramone Diaz and Raul Rodriguez," Agent Williams said.

"You think his wife is in on this?" ask a uniformed officer.

"Not in the slightest; she doesn't have a clue."

"How can you be so sure?"

"I saw the agony in her eyes," Agent Williams replied. "I'll talk with her when the time is right. You stay away from her, Sergeant."

"Yeah...sure."

Debra grasped the big man by the shoulder, spinning him around in a classic karate fashion.

Glaring up at his face, she said, "I'm not kidding here, John. Understand?"

"You just assaulted a uniformed officer of the law."

"Not yet, I haven't," the lady with a 10th degree Black Belt in Tae Kwon Do, replied. "You really want the boys down at the precinct to hear about how I kicked your ass?"

The swat team members snickered.

Chapter Twenty-Five

Nueva Gerona

Alone XS-1 helicopter lifted from the San Antonia de Banus Airfield. The Stealth flying machine headed north at 400 miles per hour into the darkness. When it left Cuban air space, the pilot flipped a switch, activating a radio beacon.

At the same time, two F-16 fighters left the naval air station on Boca Chica Key, flying south at 500 miles per hour.

The aircraft met five minutes later over the Straits of Florida. The gray colored F-16's banked and slowed to 400 miles per hour, escorting the sleek black helicopter with short wings to the Key West Airport.

"All aircraft, commercial as well as private, are advised there is a five mile no fly zone in and around Key West International until 1930 hours," the voice said calmly from the Key West air traffic tower.

"You're not serious," a private jet pilot on approach from Marathon said with irritation.

"Couldn't be more serious, unless you want to argue with an F-16. Maintain current altitude and follow American Airlines 3437 in our ten mile holding pattern over the Atlantic until further notice."

***

"Ouch!" exclaimed Danielle. One of the men wearing a Tommy Bahama shirt grasped her firmly by the arm and hurried through the white picket gate into a black Suburban with the passenger door open, waiting in the wrong lane with the engine running. The second man wearing a Tommy Bahama shirt came holding Chloe's hand, walking rapidly. Stanley followed down the sidewalk. Richard Fortin walked behind Stanley, carrying a shotgun.

The Suburban with thick glass windows drove west from 817 White Street. A police car, its red and blue overhead lights flashing, blocked the intersection at Truman Avenue and then followed the Suburban speeding through the streets. At First Street, a second police car blocked the South Roosevelt intersection. The trip to Key West International Airport took five minutes.

Chloe whimpered between her parents who were hugging as the big black vehicle sped northeast on Roosevelt.

"Isn't this fun!" Danielle said to her daughter. "Like a Disney ride, honey."

Danielle looked at Stanley.

"Where ARE we going?" she asked.

"Some place safe, that's all I know. Some place safe, honey."

"I hate this."

"Me, too."

"Guess we're flying," Stanley said, as the Suburban turned left on the airport drive.

Two homeless veterans watched the black Suburban with a police escort speed past.

"I didn't know the president was in town," the one man said slowly to the other man who was going through a green metal dumpster.

"Me either. Had one question for him," the dumpster veteran replied.

The Suburban pulled around the terminal and drove onto the runway just as the black helicopter settled on the tarmac.

"I can run without you holding my arm," Danielle snapped at the Tommy Bahama man.

Quinn O'Malley walked alongside Chloe.

Richard grasped Stanley by the back of his shirt when Stanley staggered a little while they ran towards the helicopter.

"Dizzy when I stand up fast."

"I know the feeling; got hit once by a heavy-weight," Richard laughed.

"Me, too," Stanley replied.

Leaning back in her seat, Danielle looked at the ceiling and read the words painted in large red letters over her head: TRUE BELIEVERS.

"OH MY GOD!" she shouted over the noise. "CARLA RODE IN ONE OF THESE WHEN SHE WAS RESCUED!"

Quinn reached over and patted her thigh.

"Your turn, Danielle."

He leaned close to Chloe. "You're the only nine year old who has ever ridden in one of these fantastic flying machines. Just wait until you tell your friends about this trip with Uncle Quinn!"

Quinn O'Malley looked at Stanley.

"You get your wish, my friend. We're going to Cuba."

Stanley grinned.

"Fidel's place…Nueva Gerona"

"You're going to love this place," Stanley said to Danielle. "It's where I met President Castro the first time."

"You mean this is where you and the guys met with the Mexican cartel? Just great!"

"You'll see. Probably safer than the White House, and a much better view!"

The circling F-16's escorted the XS-1 to Cuban air space. They wagged their wings and turned back.

***

Thirty minutes after leaving Key West, the helicopter settled gently on the landing pad.

"It's beautiful here," Danielle said, looking at the lighted compound.

A 1969 Tatra idled a short distance away. The passenger doors opened and Fidel Castro stood up. Dr. Marco Gonzalez climbed out from the back seat. Side by side, the

President of Cuba and his personal physician walked towards the helicopter passengers.

With a little difficulty, Fidel knelt on one knee.

"You have grown to be a beautiful young lady, Chloe Norma, like your mother," Fidel said.

Chloe did a little curtsy and extended her hand.

"I have been looking forward to meeting you, Mr. President. My mom and dad have told me all about you."

He stood up from kneeling with even more difficulty, waving away help, smiling at Danielle.

"You look even more beautiful than you did for the wedding at Truman's White House."

Danielle started to extend her right hand and then extended both arms and embraced Fidel, squeezing him tightly.

"Thank you so much. Thank you for protecting us," she said, looking up.

"You can hide in plain sight here, Danielle, for as long as you need. No one can hurt you here, and I know this first hand." He smiled. "And," he continued, "When this problem is resolved, I hope you and your husband will accept my long-standing offer to stay and work with Dr. Gonzalez."

"Thank you."

Fidel Castro turned and faced Stanley McMillen.

"You look a little worse for wear, my friend."

"You've grown a few more gray hairs yourself, Mr. President."

"That I cannot deny, Stanley. Welcome back. I am sorry to hear all you have endured recently. Dr. Gonzalez will tune you up in short order."

"Thank you."

"And then you and Danielle may help me."

"It will be our honor."

"I have a private tutor here to school Chloe," Fidel said, looking down at the beaming nine-year-old girl wearing a yellow dress with little blue flowers.

Chapter Twenty-Six

Stop Peeling This Onion

Quinn O'Malley had flown most of the night, thinking about life and his friends—all subsequent to the chance meeting with Danielle and Stanley one drinking night in the Green Parrot ten years ago, and how that meeting had changed everything for a lot of lives.

...not a chance that was a pure coincidence...

Quinn smiled, listening to the Lear's twin turbines whine, and he dozed.

The plane few north...

Richard Elmore Fortin slept while they flew.

A *CLOSED FOR INVENTORY* sign flapped a little, stapled to the front door of Poor Joe's.

...inventory indeed...

Quinn O'Malley smiled, opening the door, peeking in.

The long poker table had family style heaps of hash browns, bacon, sausages—both link and patties—scrambled eggs with little pieces of ham and mushrooms, and Dora's famous vanilla bean pancakes.

Carafes of dark coffee and warm maple syrup rested at both ends.

Timothy, Carla, Pete, Wayne, Doug, Katie, Wendell, Ralph, Rose, Machete with Little Miss at his side, and Doctors McCaferty, Smith, Fox, and Varner looked up as they walked in.

Dora carried two mugs to the table for them.

"Two cubes à La Perruche just like you like, Quinn," Dora said, smiling.

"You know I like it sweet, Dora."

"And, a double shot of Dr. Daniels in yours, Richard."

Richard reached out and squeezed her hand.

"You don't forget a thing, do you?"

"Best you remember that, Richard."

Quinn inhaled deeply and exhaled slowly from the end of the long table.

"The McMillen's are safe. They're staying at Fidel Castro's private villa on the Isle of Youth, being guarded by Cuban Special Forces and the True Believers. Fidel even has two naval destroyers circling the island and Air Force jets patrolling...just like when he's there."

"...Like when we were there," Timothy interjected.

"Fidel told me after that meeting that he admired Stanley for his bravery. And after talking with Dr. Blue, who told him that Stanley was the best critical care nurse he had ever met, he's been trying to talk Stanley and Danielle into moving to Cuba."

"Looking more likely now," Machete said a little sadly.

Vincent Bonifacio walked through the front door.

"Sorry I'm late; had to fly around a big storm in Wisconsin. I'd like something extra in my coffee, Dora."

Richard handed Vincent his mug.

"Like this?"

"What Fortin has, Dora."

"Now that we have Vincent's prescription, here's the latest update. Like I said, the McMillen's are safe and will remain in Cuba until this situation is resolved."

He paused long enough for Dora to bring a saucer piled high with à La Perruche brown cane sugar cubes. He poured a fresh cup of coffee.

"We found the blue Dodge that Steve Chase and the cartel cousins,

Ramone Diaz and Raul Rodriguez, used in Key West abandoned in an alley off Caroline Street. Not a trace or a hint of where the scumbags are hiding, and we're turning over every rock. Even the homeless vets haven't seen them, and they're aware of a big reward."

"That caught us by surprise, I'll admit," Vincent Bonifacio said. "Couldn't make a connection until the D.E.A and Alaska State Police searched Chase's house in Anchorage and found a key to an equipment and chemical warehouse Chase owned, along with a hidden room filled with pot and cocaine. He was running a distribution center for the cartel. And we think he's a consumer as well."

"Might explain a lot if he's using…psychosis," Dr. Varner ventured.

"We think so, Doctor. And why, after all these years, he's decided to come take Danielle away. He had a locked tool chest hidden with pictures of Danielle…one naked," Quinn said, looking at the table.

The anger in his eyes surprised his friends.

"Scumbag," Dora uttered from the kitchen area.

Kate put her face in her hands and shook her head.

"Stanley doing all right in Cuba?" Dr. McCaferty asked.

"Dr. Gonzalez sees him every day; talked with him yesterday. Said Stanley's dizzy spells are abating and his coordination is improving."

"Good!"

"They've recovered an estimated 5 million dollars, street value, worth of goodies from the warehouse, and, a week ago, another stash in the rafters above the garage," Quinn said. "The state has seized the warehouse and Chase's home; going up for public auction next month."

"What about his family? He's got a wife and kids, doesn't he?" Kate asked.

Quinn answered, "Mrs. Chase was served eviction papers last Tuesday."

"It's not her fault."

"No, Kate, it isn't. This is how the state punishes drug agents and distributors. This isn't her fault. The lead D.E.A. agent told me last week that Belvia Chase is completely innocent and in shock."

"What's his name?"

"Whose?"

"The D.E.A. agent."

"Debra Williams."

"Can I have her number?"

Quinn ripped the corner off the paper placemat and wrote a phone number. He handed it to Ralph who handed it down the table.

"What you got in mind, Pastor?" Quinn asked.

Katherine Kennedy McGinnis locked eyes with Quinn O'Malley while she spoke without blinking, "I have watched this whole thing unfold like a *Nightmare on Elm Street* horror movie, Quinn. We almost lost Stanley, who is hiding under guard in Cuba; I sat by his bed with Danielle, feeling the horrible agony in her soul."

Kate paused, but never blinked.

"We've got to stop peeling this onion; we do not need to see what lies beneath the next layer; we need to stop this tragedy right now. I'm calling this Debra Williams and I'm flying to

Anchorage. I'll bring Belvia Chase and her children back if that's what needs to be done, Quinn. No more innocent agony, no more senseless suffering," the pastor with a law degree from Duke, said with resolution, her green eyes glistening.

"I'm going with you," Richard Elmore Fortin said, winking at her husband with his good eye.

Doug winked back.

"I kinda was counting on it," she replied. "Doug will stay with the children."

"Vincent and I are coming along, too, Katie. God bless you, girl. We're coming along,"

Quinn cleared his throat several times and drank a gulp of sweet dark coffee.

"You call Agent Williams and tell her that we are flying up tomorrow in my plane," he said, pointing at the scribbled telephone number.

"What about her husband? What about the cartel, the cousins?" Doug asked. He reached under the table for his wife's hand. His hand was shaking a little, but Katie's hand was not.

"I think the D.E.A. is hoping they show up in Anchorage," Quinn said. "And, so am I."

"I'm going with you," Carla said.

"Me too," Rose added.

Chapter Twenty-Seven

Alien Lizards

Five-foot waves nearly swamped the rubber dingy in the moonless dark. Steve Chase and the cartel cousins lurched through the white-capped waves, Steve trying to follow a compass illuminated by Raul Rodriguez's dim flashlight. Ramone Diaz vomited violently. Six miles from

Key West, the bottom of the rubber dingy bounced against a reef twice, and then they were in the Gulf of Mexico.

A Howaldtswerke-Deutsche Werft German submarine idled on the surface, twin diesel engines recharging its batteries, the crew waiting for their bosses. The dingy approached the submarine and hit it, nearly capsizing. Two swimmers dressed in wetsuits jumped into the choppy water, holding the dingy and assisting the three men up the rope ladder. Then a gunner shot the dingy full of holes with a 50-caliber machine gun that had been retrofitted after the cartel purchased the sub from the Turkish Navy.

Hatches closed, the 200-foot submarine quietly sank beneath the Gulf of Mexico, seven miles from shore.

Lights dimmed when the power switched from diesel to electric batteries. A dim yellow glow, coming from the bulb filaments, discombobulated Steven Chase's orientation, his chemically- broken brain synapses wildly searching for reality.

The space felt more cramped than he had anticipated in a spacecraft of this magnitude. And he did not like the smell of fuel oil. The tinnitus from the electric motors became unbearable, even after he stuffed shredded toilet paper into both ears.

And the aliens were speaking in their foreign language. The short one with blue skin at the helm pointed at him and laughed. Then all eight laughed, except for the two that had been in the dingy with him. They did not laugh, but sneered in his direction, plotting his murder.

The taller of the two plotting his murder walked in his direction and when he was close enough, Steve could see his red neon eyes were glowing with hatred and that he had a lizard's face with green scales. When the lizard opened his mouth, a forked snake's tongue whipped out.

Steve fingered the cold metal Smith and Wesson in his wet jacket pocket. His finger caressed the trigger.

…a little closer and I'll blow your lizard head off…

BANG…BANG…lizard blood and green brains splattered on the spacecraft ceiling. The lizard fell down. Steve felt the knife thrown by the blue-faced alien lodge in his belly, but it did not hurt. He calmly walked closer to the aliens, shooting them all, one by one.

…a little nap will help…a little rest…

He wobbled through the narrow hallway to the bunks. On his back, with a switchblade protruding from his belly, Steve fell asleep.

…soon as I get home, Danielle will love me…

The German made submarine traveled aimlessly at 20 knots for hours. At 10 p.m. it bounced gently on the ocean floor several times. Then it rested quietly in the Gulf of Mexico, halfway between Key West and New Orleans.

At 2017 hours, the submarine imploded.

Chapter Twenty-Eight

Some Sort of Angel

Debra Williams loved Johnny Knotts immensely. They met at a dance during their junior year at the University of Washington in Seattle, she working towards a master's in social work with a minor in Spanish, while Johnny studied pre-med. They dated exclusively following the first dance that night. Her heart would pound hard every time he kissed her, and Johnny felt quivery and his skin would tingle every time she caressed him and teasingly smooched him all over his body.

"Let's get married right after I pass the boards," he had said one night, and that was their plan, a secret pact between them.

How he had gotten the heroin or who injected Johnny with a lethal overdose never was discovered. Debra had been interrogated on several occasions and her dorm room searched by Campus Police, State Troopers, and a D.E.A. agent, to no avail. No evidence of drugs was found in Johnny's apartment either.

"He never used drugs," Debra said to the D.E.A special agent, standing in the hallway outside her dorm room.

"Well, he did at least once," the special agent answered, "but you're right, there are no needle marks anywhere else on his body, and his drug screen came up negative for other drugs, just a lethal level of opiates."

Debra and the D.E.A. female special agent stared at each other.

"I believe you, Debra. And it makes no sense to me that a young man with a 4.0 GPA about to start med school...." Her voice tapered away softly. "This makes no sense. I am very sorry for your loss. That's what we are trained to say. Sorry for your loss, Debra."

She hugged Debra.

"I'm going to submit this as an open criminal investigation, young lady, not as an accidental overdose."

"Thank you."

Debra did not date anyone. For the next three years, she studied and slept.

Nine days following her graduation with a Masters of Social Work, Debra drove to the U.S Department of Justice located in downtown Seattle and walked into the Drug Enforcement office.

"I want to apply for a job as a special agent," she said to the young lady behind the bulletproof glass in the reception room.

Ten days later she returned for an interview.

"It says here that you have a masters in social work, a minor in Spanish, and that your intention was to join the Peace Corps," the gray bearded regional D.E.A. director, wearing wire-rim glasses, said from his desk. He paged through a file, looking up at Debra from time to time.

"So, why this change?"

She inhaled deeply, took several steps towards a green chair with metal legs, and dragged it behind the director's desk.

Debra sat next to the startled man.

"My lover was murdered by heroin."

The director stared at her flashing hazel eyes.

"I'm going to dedicate my life to sparing others from this awful agony I have in my soul. That is the reason, sir."

The regional director leaned back in his office chair, studying Debra.

"When would you like to start training?"

"Tomorrow."

***

Now nearly ten years later, Debra Williams waited in her office on the second floor of the old Federal Building located on West Fourth Street in Anchorage.

A pastor by the name of Katherine Kennedy McGinnis had phoned her yesterday, requesting a meeting.

Then her sectional director had called from Seattle, saying that an acquaintance of his by the name of Quinn O'Malley had called, asking for special consideration, that he owed

O'Malley a favor, and that a small group would be flying from Big Bay to Anchorage on a Lear jet owned by O'Malley.

"What kind of favor?" she had asked her director.

He had paused for almost 30 seconds before he answered.

"There is a shadow Special Forces known as the True Believers…former Green Berets, Navy Seals, French Foreign Legion, Cuban Honor Guard, and a few Israelis, as best we know. No one is certain where, they are based, but we think in Cuba with a base in Canada, too. They are not for hire, as best we can find out. But they are ardent enemies of the drug cartels in Central and South America. Fidel Castro hates drug dealers every bit as much as you do, Debra. Quinn O'Malley, who purports to be a charter boat captain in Key West, is their leader. He and Castro went to law school together. The True Believers saved the lives of three agents four years ago, just showing up without notice during a cartel ambush in El Paso. They're a fearless bunch Debra…and we owe them.

"I like them already," Debra said.

"You are about to meet O'Malley, a lady named Rose, a fellow by the name of

Vincent Bonifacio, along with the pastor, and a couple of her friends. Just listen to them."

"Yes, sir."

***

Debra stood from behind her desk when the group led by Kate walked into her office. Kate looked at Debra and stopped walking. Everyone stopped and watched the two ladies looking at each other.

"Hello, Kate," Debra said. "I feel like I know you."

"Wondered if we would meet, in this life," Kate responded. "It's wonderful to see you, again."

They simply stared for several moments while everyone in the room looked on, wondering.

Then two ageless friends hugged on earth for the first time.

"I want to help Belvia Chase if she needs it, Debra. We are here to help her."

Debra motioned for everyone to sit, and she sat with Kate on her right.

"She needs help. Everything she owns has been seized and will be auctioned. She has no idea how to proceed. Her parents are deceased. Her only sibling, a brother, was killed in the first Gulf War. She's alone and scared."

"She's completely innocent of anything her husband did." Debra continued, "I've rented her a couple of motel rooms." She stopped and rubbed her forehead. "Her husband is a son-of-a-bitch."

"*That* we know, Debra. Steve Chase tried to kill a good friend of ours in Big Bay last month."

"Why?"

"His high school sweetheart is Stanley's wife. He started calling her a couple of months ago."

Debra looked at the people in her office with wide, alarmed eyes. She pulled open a desk drawer and retrieved an envelope. Slowly she spread pictures on her desk.

"Is this Stanley's wife?"

They approached the desk.

Quinn and Vincent turned away when they saw the naked picture of young Danielle, standing on the beach under a Christmas palm.

Kate began breathing hard through pursed lips.

"Yes, that's Danielle. She's Stanley's wife. Does Mrs. Chase know her husband had these?" Kate asked.

"She does now."

"Let's go meet her and those poor children. We're thrown together in this dark and awful time and we both know it's not by accident. No more awful pain. We need to rescue them from the demons in their world."

"Let's go," Debra replied, and she put the pictures back in the desk drawer.

"I think I will call you guys 'The Demon Slayers'," she said, looking at the assembled in her office above the courtroom below.

Kate looked at Debra through the red curls dangling on her forehead.

"We have known each other for a very long time, my friend," Debra said.

"Long before we got our tickets for mother earth," Kate said.

Quinn O'Malley looked at Vincent and winked.

Carla and Rose shrugged. Then they hugged.

***

Belvia Chase opened the dirty white motel room door and looked out with reddened eyes.

"Hi, Belvia, how you doing?"

"Not so good, Debra."

"Help is here," Debra said. She stood aside and gently pushed Katie into the room filled with gray and stormy clouds and three kids watching Bugs Bunny-Roadrunner cartoons on a 21 inch black and white Motorola television.

"Agent Debra is paying for this, can you believe it…how kind she is?" Belvia said to Kate.

"Yes, Belvia, I can."

"Who are you?"

"My name is Kate."

"This is Carla, Rose, Vincent, Richard, and Quinn," she continued, pointing through the open door to the sidewalk. "I'm a pastor, and these friends came with me to see if we can help you in any way."

"Are you guys missionaries or something?"

"In a way, that is exactly right, Belvia, and we're here to help you."

Belvia Chase went from person to person, looking at each face with a questioning look, saying nothing. She stopped when she reached Richard, looking at the scar on his face.

"How'd you know I needed help?"

Quinn O'Malley started to say something, and Debra cut him off, "I have been friends with Pastor Katie for a very long time, Belvia. I sent her a message."

"First you find me a place to stay while the damn Feds take my house away from me—sorry Deb—then you call your friend. I think you must be some sort of angel."

Debra Williams laughed. "You wouldn't say that if you saw my bar tab at the F Street Station."

"I've no idea how we are going to live or how we can even exist, Kate. If it hadn't been for Debra, we'd be living at the homeless shelter."

Belvia turned towards her children who now stared at the group from the couch.

"This is Norah," she said, pointing towards the oldest child.

"I'm eight," Norah said.

"My name is Miranda. I'm almost seven," the little blond girl said.

"My name is Edmond Steven Chase. I'm five."

Kate sat on the floor in front of the rust colored couch and looked up.

"You guys wanna get outa here and move to a real cool town with lots of kids your own age and a great Sunday school, too?"

"Yeah!" they cheered in unison.

"Well, Mom?" she asked, looking up from the floor. "Want a plane ride away from this mess and the start of a new life?"

"Where?"

"Big Bay."

"Never heard of it."

"You're going love it. Take it from a girl raised in Boston; you're going to love it. And, it just so happens the Methodist Church owns a house that is vacant…perfect for your family."

"When?"

"Tonight; we can leave tonight." Quinn O'Malley said. "Right after we all go over to the F Street Station. They serve the best halibut salad with blue cheese. Right Special Agent Williams?"

"That is correct, Captain O'Malley."

The group helped pack the family's few belongings into white garbage bags and two cardboard boxes and stowed them in the back of the black Suburban.

"Oh boy, we're going to a bar!" shouted Norah as the children climbed into the back seat, squeezing between Rose and Carla.

Quinn climbed into the front bucket seat, next to Debra.

"If I was a younger man, I would camp on your doorstep, I think," he said while pulling the seatbelt across his lap.

Debra's head snapped to the right, peering at the man with a missing front tooth smiling at her.

"What's age got to do with it, Quinn?"

Belvia sat next to Richard.

"I feel safe when I'm next to you, sir."

"You should," he replied. "Please call me Richard."

Chapter Twenty-Nine
Knight in Shining Armor

"To be honest," Danielle said, walking slowly next to Stanley on the paths in the hillside garden around the villa, "I'm surprised that Richard didn't stay here with us."

"I asked him to keep an eye on things back home. He wanted to stay."

"Oh."

Stanley pointed at a destroyer slowly cruising in the Gulf of Batabano and then at a helicopter gunship making chop chopping sounds while circling the hilltop.

"His enemies couldn't hurt him here. Fidel feels safe here…we sure are, honey."

He stooped over and picked a pink hibiscus then dropped to one knee and extended the flower towards Danielle.

"If you had it to do all over, knowing our lives would be like this, would you?"

Danielle dropped to both knees in the dust.

"You are my knight in shining armor. You make me laugh. You make me happy. You and I made Chloe. You have introduced me to characters that most people only see in the movies. Absolutely I would. I came looking for you, honey. Would you?"

Stanley pushed his forehead against Danielle's, noses tip to tip, and their eyes wide open wide.

"Yes."

The helicopter flew overhead and lower.

"I think the guy in the open door took our picture," Stanley said.

"Want to really give him something to photograph?" Danielle said, looking up and waving.

"You're a naughty one."

"You know that better than anyone, mister."

They walked side-by-side back towards the house.

"Why do you think Castro is doing this?" Danielle asked. "He hardly knows us."

Stanley pointed towards the top story of the villa, a large round room with a copper roof and tinted windows extending from the floor to the ceiling.

"That's the room where we met with the Mexican cartel godfather. The relationship between Fidel and Quinn astounded me. They embraced when Fidel entered the room, and I could feel adoration and absolute trust between them. They even finish each other's sentences.

One time—the time Fidel first asked if we would consider coming to help—it was just Fidel, Quinn, and me sitting up there, smoking cigars." Stanley pointed to a deck extending from the round room. "He said to me that Quinn had saved his life in the early days of the revolution."

They stopped walking and Stanley faced his wife, placing a hand on each of her shoulders.

"I think he is taking care of us because of Quinn. And I think he's doing this because, for some reason, he likes you and me a lot. Sometimes it feels like an aging father who is trying to make amends, and we are his chosen children."

"Oh, my, that explains a lot. I meant to tell you, starting last Monday, a bus brings the entire 5th grade girls class from José Marti

Elementary. They hold classes here, Stanley. I asked one teacher why, and she said, 'Because our president does not want your daughter taught in a vacuum; this way our children will learn English faster, and your Chloe will learn our Spanish.'"

"See what I mean?" Stanley said.

"Now you see how silly your question is, honey? Look at all the adventure I'd have missed if I had just settled for Steve Chase."

Stanley laughed.

"He certainly added some excitement to this chapter of our lives."

"Because of him...jeez...and now it almost feels like house arrest. This is beautiful, but it's not safe to go to town or go out to eat. I'm sorry."

"They'll find him. Quinn and the guys will find him. Then we'll go home. When the time is right for us, we'll come back."

"There you go again, making my heart smile. Would I do it again? You're a silly boy, Stanley James McMillen."

"Just to help put things into perspective, there is a prison in town," Stanley said, pointing down the hill towards the city, "that big round cement building. Fidel was a prisoner there in 1955. Quinn O'Malley busted him out. Look at how all that turned out."

"And here we are, Castro's guests," Danielle said, squeezing her husband's hand as tight as she could.

Chapter Thirty
A Very Fast Gift

"Yesterday the Coast Guard found a rubber dingy with a Johnson outboard washed up on the coral reef in the Gulf," Quinn O'Malley said on the phone. "That's why we can't find Steve Chase and the cartel cousins; must have had a boat waiting on the other side of the reef. The dingy was shot full of large caliber holes."

"They use mounted fifty calibers," Debra Williams answered.

"If they were still in Key West, we'd have found them. Every homeless vet, bartender, grocery store clerk, bouncer, lady of the evening, and city employee has been looking, hoping for a secret payday."

"You do that too, huh? How're Belvia and her kids? Have you heard?"

"Haven't for a couple of days."

"It might have been a submarine, Quinn."

"Didn't know they had subs."

"One of those classified secrets on a need-to-know basis."

"How big?"

"We know the cartel purchased three German made diesel electric subs—two hundred footers—from the Turkish Navy."

"Seems like that would be something you guys would have shared."

"The director doesn't want the cartel to know that we know they have subs."

"Kind of hard to have the Coast Guard and Navy looking for something that doesn't exist. "

"We have plans to intercept a sub filled with cocaine in the near future."

"This a secure line, Deb?"

"Of course."

"Good, I don't want you fired."

"I'd be homeless, Quinn. Probably have to come to Key West and move in with you."

Quinn laughed. "I'm pretty loose-lipped, Deb."

"You better not, old man."

"Crossed my mind that you and your guys might want to take a look around the Gulf some night with your flying machines that don't exist."

"You heard, huh?"

"Do they really go 400 miles per hour?"

"They do. Quite a thrill, flying 50 feet over the water… I'll have Richard take you for a ride sometime."

"He's a pilot?"

"He is the best there ever was, Deb, unbelievable. No depth perception now since he lost his right eye, but he'd love to take you on a ride."

"Belvia sure was clinging to him at the airport."

"Timothy told me last week that he thinks they're in love."

"Really!"

"Richard told Timothy he wished Steve Chase would show up. That's Richard's way of saying it."

"Oh my."

"Katie and Doug are throwing a welcoming party for Belvia and her children at Poor Joe's a week from Saturday. I'm flying up for it.

Would you like if I flew over and picked you up and we go together?"

"I have that weekend off. Quinn, I'd love to go. What's Poor Joe's?"

"The Big Bay rendition of F Street Station; you'll love it and the folks there."

"One more question, Deb. What was that between you and Katie in your office?"

"I think we were best friends from another time, Quinn. Haven't you had that happen, meeting an old friend for the very first time?"

"I think I just have, Debra."

"Quinn, it's 5000 miles from Key West to Anchorage."

"I know. Just got a new jet," Quinn replied, "Gulfstream S-21, goes 1500 miles an hour. I can be in Anchorage in three and half hours, non-stop!"

"I'm excited to see you."

***

She watched the sleek white jet with a needle nose circle once on approach to Anchorage International and then land. Quinn bounded out with a grin. When they were close, he spread his arms wide and they embraced.

Debra grasped Quinn's left hand. They strolled towards the jet. Quinn pulled her suitcase. "I researched this jet; it was a joint venture between Gulfstream and a Russian company. They never made it, Quinn. These planes were never built."

"Ain't it something, submarines that don't exist, helicopters that you can't see on radar, and private jets that hit Mach 2…never built? Let's go to Big Bay, Deb. It'll take less than three hours!"

"It looks more like a living room," Debra said, looking through the door. She felt the soft leather and took a deep breath.

"These are all recliners, and when you swivel around, there is a table that folds out from the wall like a rail dining car," Quinn said. "We're going to have a picnic on the way to Big Bay."

Flying at forty thousand feet, facing Quinn across the table, Debra said, "I have to ask, how does a one boat charter boat captain afford something like this?"

"A gift, Deb; this is a gift from a dear friend in the oil business. We were able to rescue his wife and two sons from a group of Saudi nutcases who were threatening to behead them unless an outrageous ransom was paid. Six of the bravest men on God's green earth took a commercial flight from Havana to Riyadh, then a corporate chopper two miles to a walled compound near Medina. They rescued all three, shooting the zealots using silencers, and were gone in seven minutes."

"Wow!"

"He had this plane built for us as a thank you and to allow a rapid response any place in the world. It's a prototype, the only one flying."

"Us?"

"Now you're playing cop with me."

"The True Believers."

"Exactly."

"Why that name?"

"We believe, Deb. We believe we can. Seemed like a good name. Scares the shit out of the bad guys."

"From what I hear, it should. This is a beautiful plane, Quinn."

She sipped a cup of tea and placed it back in the saucer.

....Johnny curled on the floor, a syringe and the needle protruding from his left arm...his kind eyes open...no blinking...

"Do you worry about repercussions from the bad guys?" Debra asked.

Quinn pushed the plates to the end of the table. He reached across and held both of Debra's hands tightly.

"This is the first time I've talked about this," he said.

Debra could hardly hear him over the sound of the engines.

"In 1955 my college friend, Fidel Castro, was incarcerated in one of Fulgencio Batista's prisons. I bribed a guard to tell me where in the prison Fidel was being held. Then, on a Sunday night, three of us attacked with dynamite and grenades. We broke him out. Five days later, my fiancé was murdered by Batista's secret police."

He paused. Debra felt his hands turning cold.

...bloody bits of foam rubber sticking to the walls...pillow feathers...her face gone...

"They murdered my Maria Chanchez as she slept. Three cowards shot her in her bed with machine guns. Batista claimed she was a communist spy. Maria was the most loving soul I have ever met. Since that day, I have no fear of death; it will be a reunion, I think. Since that day, it doesn't matter."

"I'm sorry that happened in your life."

"Shit happens, Deb. You know that."

"Yes," she replied.

Debra stood, and leaning over the table, kissed Quinn on the lips.

"I'm happy we have found each other," she said.

"I'm happy, too."

"How'd you lose that front tooth?"

"Lost it the night we rescued Fidel. Never wanted to fix it, after Maria."

"It's time, now."

"I think so, too."

Chapter Thirty-One
Ventricular Fibrillation

A large brown helicopter landed on the villa helipad. The pilot, wearing a Cuban Air Force uniform, removed his sunglasses and switched the twin turbines off.

"Stay here," Stanley said to Danielle, looking into the rising sun at two tall men in uniform walking briskly towards the villa.

Stanley opened the door from the lower level and walked towards the young men.

"Doctor Gonzalez sends for you," the one wearing a military hat said in broken English.

"He has need for you and the wife to help."

"Please hurry, get the bags," the other man said.

"Suitcases?" Stanley asked. "Where are we going?"

"Cardenas. Hospital de Cardenas."

The man wearing an officer's hat handed Stanley a sealed note. Danielle approached and touched his arm. He pealed back the seal and unfolded the note.

Fidel hospitalized. Inferior Wall Myocardial Infarction last night. Ventricular Fibrillation twice…Hospital de Cardenas ill equipped but the president too unstable for transfer to Havana. I need you and Danielle Marco.

"I'll pack our travel cases and get Chloe ready."

"I need my briefcase…upstairs. Meet you in the living room."

Twenty minutes later the helicopter lifted, rotated to the north, and flew over the Caribbean Sea for the 3-hour trip to Cardenas.

"What's that?' Chloe ask her daddy as he punched a series of numbers on a yellow triangular shaped phone.

"A special phone, honey. I can call Uncle Quinn anyplace in the world on this phone."

"I want one," she replied, leaning closer. "It's ordenado!"

"It's what?"

"It's neat, Daddy…ordenado!"

"I need you to give me Spanish lessons, honey."

"El gusto es mio."(My pleasure)

"Whatever." Stanley rubbed her curly hair.

***

Quinn pulled a yellow phone from his pocket, borrowed Debra's reading glasses from the top of her head, and read the rectangular screen on the back of his triangular phone.

"Stanley, you guys ok?"

"Fidel had a heart attack last night, Quinn. Doctor Gonzalez sent a helicopter to pick us up."

"Where's Fidel?"

"Cardenas."

"They taking him to Havana?"

"He's not stable enough to transfer." Stanley hesitated, and then continued, "He fibrillated twice last night, Quinn. We're on our way up there right now."

"I'm in Big Bay, Stanley; be down this afternoon. Thanks."

Quinn O'Malley stared at the yellow phone on the poker table in Poor Joe's. All the people around the table stopped talking and stared, reading the bad news in his eyes.

Debra reached to her right and rubbed his Hemingway beard. She moved her fingers under his chin and slowly turned his face towards hers to see absolute agony.

"I don't know what just happened, but I'm going with you. Let's go."

"It's Fidel," Quinn said. "He's very sick. That cannot leave this room."

Quinn leaned back in his chair, looking up at the neon clock above the bar.

"We leave now, I can be with him by two."

"Let's go," Debra said, rubbing his hand.

"Fidel and I have been through everything you can imagine. Long ago we made a pact." He rubbed his forehead. "Damn it!"

***

Two armored personnel carriers with machine guns manned, idled at the entrance to the single story cement building painted yellow with a green stripe at the roofline. Clusters of soldiers carrying automatic weapons circled the building.

"HOSPITAL de CARDENAS," Stanley read out loud, looking at the black lettering above the entrance.

Stanley and Danielle left the car, walking behind the tall Air Force pilots towards the hospital.

A large bald man, trim not fat, held his right hand up and entered into earnest conversation with the pilot wearing an officer's hat.

"That man doesn't trust who we are, Daddy. He told our soldier that no one stays at President Castro's villa. He is not going to let us in the hospital."

Stanley walked towards the large man.

"Do you speak English?"

"A little."

Stanley removed Doctor Gonzalez's note from his shirt pocket.

"This is a note that Doctor Marco Gonzalez sent, asking for help. He is the president's personal physician."

"I do not read the English"

Stanley motioned towards Chloe.

"Can you read this to the major?" he asked, looking at the big man's insignia.

"Fidel hospitalizado. Inferior anoche Muro infarto de miocardio. Fibrilación Ventricular dos veces…Hospital de Cárdenas mal equipado, pero el presidente demasiado inestable para su traslado a La Habana. Te necesito y Danielle Marco."

Stanley listened with amazement. Danielle squeezed his arm and whispered. "She is brilliant, like you, honey. Her Spanish teacher told me Chloe has learned more during this year than any first year student she has tutored over her twenty-three year career. She sees a word and hears it, and that's all it takes…one time."

"Good job, honey."

"Maybe you wrote this," the big major said, taking the letter from Chloe and looking at

Stanley.

"He gave it to me," Stanley said, pointing.

"Air Force, they can be purchased, amigo."

"Let's get Dr. Gonzalez. He'll vouch for us; he sent for us," Danielle interjected.

"I am in charge here, not that Doctor Gonzalez."

Stanley's skin prickled, along with the urge to pee, accompanied by a faint vinegar taste, waiting for the bell to ring signaling round one. He moved close to the big man, almost touching, eyes level with the major, not blinking, staring a cold stare.

"I would not want to be in your shoes if the president dies and we were not allowed to help because of your ignorant ego, Major."

"Is that a threat?"

"It is a promise. Our dear friend, Quinn O'Malley will explain in more descriptive words that I am sure you will understand when he arrives soon."

The big major stepped back and glanced at Danielle.

"He is my Uncle," Chloe said with a big smile.

The major looked at the note he could not read for several seconds.

"Any friend of Captain O'Malley is welcome here. Please enter."

"¿De verdad es tu tío? (Is he really your uncle)," the major asked Chloe.

"Sí, y se casó con mi papá y mamá en su luna de miel." (Yes, and he married my dad and mom on their honeymoon.)

***

The blue-colored, 1970's vintage cardiac monitor made irregular beep-beeping sounds while a little bright dot scrolled up and down from left to right on the light yellow screen with each heartbeat. Doctor Gonzalez and a young nurse with her black hair pulled back into a ponytail were leaning over a metal table against the wall in the small room, reviewing the morning lab tests and vital signs graphic sheet. Doctor Gonzalez looked up when Stanley and Danielle walked in with Chloe.

"I'm happy you are here," he said, softly. "We had to defibrillate again this morning—five times. CPR for seven minutes. Feared we had lost him."

"Third episode?" Stanley asked.

"Yes. Switched from a lidocaine drip to bretylate."

The two men hugged.

"You are looking much better, Stanley."

The young nurse watched.

"Hi, Marco," Danielle said quietly. They embraced.

"Really need your help; I'm all alone here. This room is the best we can manage for a CCU; no critical care nurses. Not their fault, no critical care here."

Fidel slept.

"Sedated him after the last episode."

"Why the oxygen tent, Marco? We haven't used those since the 70's."

Doctor Gonzalez smiled. "We haven't either, Stan. No air conditioning here; cooler in the tent."

"I should have known," Stanley said. "It's gotta be ninety in here."

Fidel opened his eyes and stared. Then he motioned towards Chloe and patted the bed.

"Open the tent, Marco," Fidel said.

Doctor Gonzalez unzipped the side panel.

Castro patted the bed.

"Sit here while we talk, Chloe."

Chloe glanced back at her mother. Danielle nodded *yes*.

One step up on the footstool and Chloe Norma McMillen sat on President Fidel Castro's hospital bed.

"How are your Spanish studies?" he asked in Spanish.

"I like Spanish more than English," Chloe responded in the Cuban dialect.

"Why is that?"

"It sounds sexier!"

"It does, does it? What would an eight year old know about sexier?"

Chloe giggled. "I'm nine, almost ten."

"Your parents do not speak Spanish yet?"

"Not yet."

"Whew."

"Machete Juarez told me you were very sick last year, in the hospital like I am now."

"Machete came with Little Miss and prayed for me. He would not leave my room. An angel came and kissed me. Then I woke up from a dream that I was in heaven."

"Did your angel have a name?"

"Machete called her Janet Sue."

"I met her last night, this Janet Sue. She took me to my mother, Lina. I hugged my mother. Then my chest felt like fire. Doctor Gonzalez was staring at my face."

"I've never told even my mother."

"Sometimes it's better to keep things a secret, I think. It is a beautiful place that I did not believe existed, my dear sweet child. Your Spanish is almost as good as mine."

"It sounds sexy!"

"Let's keep that a secret as well."

"I will. I think my daddy knows what it is like to die, too. He looked like it for awhile one day after the car hit him."

"Mr. O'Malley told me this as well."

"Uncle Quinn is coming here today! My daddy called him on that funny looking phone when we were flying here."

Fidel smiled.

"I knew he would. We have an agreement."

"I want one of those yellow phones someday."

"I will see to it, Chloe."

***

"Is Amiodarone available?" Stanley asked, watching short salvos of Ventricular Tachycardia on the monitor.

"Coming from Havana, should be here within the hour."

"Good. What do you think about some magnesium?"

"Good idea."

Chloe jumped down from the bed.

"He wants to talk to you, Daddy, and Mommy, too."

They leaned through the tent opening.

"You'd probably rather be in the mountains having people shoot at you," Stanley said with a grin.

"Safer…much safer and noble. Now it is clear to me why you and Danielle are in Cuba at his time. God knew I would need you. We are placed on this earth to help each other, just in case we wondered."

"I've believed that for a very long time, Mr. President," Danielle said.

"Your daughter is an angel, sent from God. You know that already, don't you?"

"Yes, we do."

"Machete is certain of this as well. He believes Chloe is his baby sister, Maria, reincarnated."

She could not resist, and leaned into the tent. Danielle kissed Fidel Castro on his pale sweaty forehead. It felt cold.

"We have been sent a very special young lady, Mr. President."

Chapter Thirty-Two

She's a Naughty One

A sense of astonishment seized Debra William's mind, walking quickly next to Quinn, after exiting the car.

Men wearing brown uniforms holding automatic weapons quickly formed a line, saluting. A large bald man standing at the end of the line near the entrance saluted crisply as they approached.

"Welcome, General."

General…what the hell…General of what…we're going to talk, buddy…

Danielle looked exactly as she had anticipated, beautiful, just an older version from the pictures in her desk drawer.

Chloe turned towards them and ran, leaping into Quinn's arms when they entered the room.

Chloe looked at Debra from Quinn's arms.

…exactly like her mom…a little clone of Danielle…

"What's your name?"

"Debra. Your Uncle Quinn has told me all about you."

"What did he say?"

"I said you are gift from God, that you are very smart, and that you are beautiful," Quinn said, lowering her to the floor. "That is what I said, and that you are studying Spanish."

"How do you like Spanish?" Debra asked.

"She says it is sexy," Fidel's muffled voice coming from the oxygen tent.

Chloe giggled.

"It is. How do you know Spanish?" Chloe said in Spanish with juvenile excitement.

"I took it in high school and college," Debra replied in Spanish.

"It will be our language. No one will understand."

Quinn laughed and winked at Debra.

Danielle turned her head slowly away from Fidel's patient chart, watching Quinn place Chloe on the floor while he walked towards the bed, and looked for the first time at Debra.

Debra stared back. The same hazel eyes, which had sparkled at her from Quinn's arms, now stared at her with love and a curiosity, peeling away the shutters that concealed secrets.

"Hi, I'm Danielle McMillen."

…can't blame Steve Chase…no wonder he never gave up…

"I'm Debra Williams. It is a pleasure to meet you. Quinn has spoken of you and your husband many times."

"How do you know Quinn?"

"I'm his girlfriend."

"You are a fortunate lady."

"Fortunate for both of us, Danielle."

"I look forward to our becoming friends, Debra."

"As do I. We have a lot to talk about."

Danielle stared without blinking before responding, her chin slightly lowered.

"I think that's true."

…shit, Stanley better never try to cheat…she's a walking truth detector…

***

His jaw muscles quivered at the sight of Fidel in the oxygen tent. Quinn stood next to Stanley, looking at his face, asking without saying a word.

"I've seen you looking worse, old man," Quinn said. He unzipped the side panel.

Fidel turned his head.

"When?"

"The morning after that night in Vinales."

"I was younger, and it was not my fault; those ladies put something in my rum, yours too, as I recall."

Quinn leaned in and collapsed, stumbling on the footstool, into the bed, hugging his best friend.

"We'll get you through this one, too," He whispered.

"We're not going to live forever, Quinn."

"True enough. I was kinda counting on a biplane ride over the Gulf with you at the controls."

Fidel smiled.

"Better get it booked, brother. The clock is ticking."

Stanley and Doctor Gonzalez stood next to the metal table covered with several layers of chipped, green paint, watching the cardiac monitor.

"Is he in chronic atrial fib?" Stanley asked.

"No, been in sinus rhythm until this last episode of VT."

"Seen that happen a lot. When do you want to cardiovert him?"

"He's rate controlled on the digitalis. Let's see if the Amiodarone converts him tonight."

"Speaking of nights, how about if I take the nightshift and Danielle takes the dayshift—twelve hour shifts—and you get some rest."

"That sounds perfect, Stanley. I'll be in the on-call room next to the Emergency Room, if you need me."

***

The nurse with the ponytail watched Stanley work in the makeshift CCU from the nurses' station. Through the open door, she watched as he changed IV bottles, made notes in the chart, and took President Castro's blood pressure.

…He is a handsome one…

A wave of fatigue hit Stanley around 3 a.m. His mind flashed to the year he graduated.

…feels like room 314 before the CCU…Damn, forgot how awful nights feel…this is a younger person's sport…

With sparkling, naughty eyes, she watched while Stanley nodded off briefly in the chair next to the green table. Almost silently, she entered the dimly lit room.

Stanley jerked when she rubbed the back of his head.

"Sorry, must have nodded off," he said while standing up.

She looked up at him, her dark eyes watching his reaction.

…she's beautiful…

"hablas español?" (Do you speak Spanish?) She asked, moving close enough to press her left breast against his arm.

"No español," Stanley replied. He looked out the door at the empty nurses' station.

She pointed through the small window towards the lighted street outside. Then bending down, her shiny black ponytail over her right shoulder, she wrote *241* and handed it to Stanley, pointing at an apartment complex across the street.

"Oh," Stanley said. He raised his left hand and pointed at his ring finger.

"Danielle," he said, pointing to the gold ring.

"Rhea," she replied, pointing at herself with a wink. She walked back to the nursing station, turned around, and smiled.

"She's a naughty one."

Stanley turned to see Fidel smiling.

"Yes sir, *that* she is."

"You handled her nicely, Stanley. I knew you would."

"Thank you," Stanley replied, looking through the window just as a man, dressed completely in black, jogged down the alley under the dim street lamp.

Chapter Thirty-Three
Like the Old Days

The bald major slowly turned the antenna trim knob while watching the signal strength needle and flipped the switch to single side band on the shortwave transmitter.

"Goaltender calling Point Man. Goaltender calling Point Man."

He waited, listening to the static.

"Goaltender calling Point Man."

"Point Man, go ahead. Goaltender."

The major squinted in the dim light at the dials, adjusting the antenna trim again.

"Big Bad Wolf and Robin Hood are in the corral."

"That is good news."

"Day of reckoning is at hand," the big man replied.

"Harvesters are en route. Will arrive in six hours."

Juan Veracruz pushed the mute button and the static from the shortwave transceiver became silent. He sat quietly in the soft chair, stroking his goatee with the fingers of his left hand. Turning slowly, he looked up from the desk, staring at the portraits on the wall illuminated by the yellow light emitted by twelve candles on the shelf below. A new portrait had been added—that of Jesus Veracruz—hanging next to his brother.

"Soon Uncle," he said, looking up at Cesar Veracruz, "very soon your nemeses will be vanquished. Soon Fidel Castro and Quinn O'Malley will die. Soon your dream of free trade in the Caribbean will be true, I promise."

***

Stanley blushed slightly when Danielle walked past the nurses' station and entered the little CCU.

Rhea stared as she passed and winked at Stanley.

"How'd the night go?" Danielle asked.

"Kinda quiet; no VT for nine hours."

"She's hitting on you, isn't she?"

"Why'd you ask something like that, honey?" Stanley replied, his blush becoming more evident.

"Come on, Stan, she stared daggers in my back when I walked by."

"You should be very proud of your husband; he is a rock," Fidel said from inside the oxygen tent. "He pointed to the wedding ring you gave him and kept repeating your name."

Danielle looked at Stanley who shrugged.

"Well, she is beautiful, Stan."

"Not even close to your league, sweetheart."

"He's stronger than I would have been," the president of Cuba said, followed by a chuckle.

***

"You awake, Doctor?" Quinn O'Malley asked, poking his head into the dark on-call room.

"Am now," replied Dr. Gonzalez. "Come in. What's up?"

"Can Fidel be moved safely?"

"When?"

"Now."

"No, not safely. Why?"

"We are going to be attacked."

***

Quinn O'Malley, Debra Williams, and Doctor Marco Gonzalez hustled past the nurses' station. Quinn closed the door after entering Castro's room.

Fidel studied the three briefly, looking from face to face, stopping on Quinn.

"Remove this tent, please," he said.

Stanley and Danielle pulled the plastic from under the mattress, collapsed the aluminum contraption like an accordion, and pushed it against the wall.

"I have seen that look before, Quinn. When are they coming?"

Danielle looked at Quinn and then Stanley, wide-eyed.

"What we have in our favor is that Major Alvarez Prieto is not a smart man," Quinn said. "He is a Major of the Regional Matanzas Battalion simply through longevity and brute force, but he is not smart."

Fidel sighed and shook his head.

"We have known for many years that Major Prieto communicates by shortwave with the Veracruz head of the Mexican drug cartel. Each day of the week a different sideband frequency is used. His mistake is using the same seven frequencies every week in the same order."

Fidel interrupted from his bed. "It is to our advantage that he is not aware that we know. Over the years, we have intercepted some of the drugs, sometimes not, just to prevent suspicions."

"Well, here is the bad news," Quinn continued.

Everyone stared. Fidel cocked his head.

"There is going to be an assassination attempt, Mr. President. The Mexican cartel is sending a hit squad to join Major Prieto and his band of loyalists. They think they have the Big Bad Wolf and Robin Hood trapped," Quinn stated, first pointing at Castro and then himself.

"When?" Stanley asked.

Danielle moved closer to her husband, putting her arm around his back.

"Tonight at the earliest. Depends when the hit squad arrives. Probably tonight, Stan. I have a taxi coming for you and Danielle at 0830 to take you to a safe house in Colon."

Danielle's body trembled against Stanley. He looked at her hazel eyes staring at him.

"You're not going, are you, honey?" she said.

Stanley looked at the floor.

"It's ok. You stay and help keep our friend alive. Chloe and I will be waiting. A taxi, Quinn, really? A taxi? Let's go to the hotel and get Chloe."

"It looks like a taxi; it's an armor-plated Mercedes. You know the driver, Danielle."

"Who?"

"Richard."

Debra Williams left the room and returned, walking quickly.

"The taxi is here. Let's go pick up Chloe. I'm going with you, Danielle."

Quinn looked at Debra and exhaled a long breath. She embraced him, squeezing tightly.

"You beat these bastards, old man. I have plans for you."

Quinn kissed the top of her curly head.

"Have I let you down yet?"

"Not in the slightest."

Danielle trembled.

"Is this enough excitement?" Stanley said, smiling through blurry eyes.

"Damn you, Stanley."

Danielle moved to Fidel's bed, straightened the sheets, and sat on the bed.

"Mr. President," she said.

His brown eyes stared back. She grasped his hand.

"I'm leaving now to protect our daughter. Otherwise, I would be staying right here at your side, next to my husband and my friends, protecting you. I only wish the rest of the world knew you the way Stanley and I know you."

"You are my true friends," he replied. "I love you and your family like my own."

Danielle leaned forward, kissing Fidel on his wet forehead. This time it felt warm.

She jumped off the bed and walked back to Stanley, kissed him on the lips, and headed towards the door with Debra. Just before leaving, she turned to face the four men.

"You better not die. I'll really be pissed." And she was gone.

***

"This must be how Davy Crockett felt," Stanley muttered.

Fidel, Marco, and Quinn looked at him.

"The Alamo," Stanley retorted.

Quinn chuckled.

"Not quite. The stupid major and the Mexicans think they have the element of surprise going for them. It is the Alamo that will provide the surprise, Stanley," Fidel said. "Someone give me a pistol. I want to go out like your Jim Bowie."

Stanley watched a short burst of Ventricular Tachycardia go across the monitor screen and glanced at Dr. Gonzalez, who nodded. Stanley slowly pushed 100 mg of Amiodarone into the president's IV line and increased the infusion rate.

"I watched a man dressed in black run down the alley early this morning, Quinn."

"Team Mongoose flew in last night, Stanley."

Fidel smiled. "They are the best of the best," he rested his head back on the pillow, "the very best, Stanley."

"They have taken up positions on adjacent rooftops: the roof of the apartment complex on one side and the office complex on the other side."

A man wearing a soiled Caribbean Soul T-shirt opened the door and entered Castro's room.

Rhea liked him even more than Stanley.

The man spoke with a South African accent.

"General, we have the perimeter secured. The lobby is now staffed with visitors. The Cantina across the street is staffed and filled with patrons."

"The owner give you trouble?"

"He agreed to a vacation, with our compliments. His family has never been to Disney World."

"Very good," Quinn said.

The South African turned to face Stanley.

"Your wife and daughter are safe."

"Thank you."

"And the gunships?" Quinn asked.

"Two ready. Can be on location ten minutes after notification. Both equipped with Gatlings and sun-lights."

Quinn smiled.

"Let the bastards come, Mr. President; let them try."

Stanley and Marco looked at Quinn, then at each other. Fidel quipped from the bed, "Now you will get to know the General I know," pointing at Quinn. "I still want a pistol."

The South African smiled. He reached into a canvas bag slung over his shoulder and retrieved a silver revolver.

"Like the old days," Quinn said.

Then the man handed Stanley and Dr. Gonzalez each a black revolver.

"Just so you can tell your grandchildren," he said with a broad smile. "You all set, General?"

Quinn patted his jacket pocket.

Chapter Thirty-Four

Like Gideon's Army

The Friday evening perch and steak special with a side of Dora's famous clam chowder had Poor Joe's packed with patrons when Vincent Bonifacio squeezed past people standing in line at the entrance.

"Hey, mister, we have a line here for a reason."

"Yeah, no cuts," added a man with a can of Schlitz in his right hand.

Vincent thought for a brief instant, decided against what crossed his mind, and pushed through towards the bar.

Timothy spotted him first and walked out from behind the bar.

"Vincent!"

"Problems, Timothy. Richard here?

"Last I saw, him and Machete were playing Old Maid at the southwest table."

"How does he do it?"

"The guys used to think he had the cards marked somehow, so they bought a new deck. Machete said, 'They smell new,' and grinned; made no difference to him."

Wendell, Chief Strait, Doug, Pete, Wayne, Richard, and Little Miss looked up when Timothy and Vincent approached the southwest table.

Machete looked up and smiled.

"You still use that Italian aftershave, Vincent," Machete said, extending his hand.

"I need to speak with Richard. Oh, what the hell. Where can we be in private, guys? "My room is the biggest," Machete said, reaching down for Little Miss.

Each man took a chair.

Timothy opened the door under the stairs.

"Hey…leasch sum damn shairs," slurred a patron.

"Free cup of clam chowder if you eat it standing," Timothy said, closing the door.

"No way to candy-coat this, fellows, and I know what is said here will not leave this room."

The old vets nodded.

"Fidel Castro had a heart attack three days ago. Dr. Gonzalez—you guys remember him from Doug's wedding—had Stanley and Danielle fly in to help with his care; seems they are in a little regional hospital that is ill-equipped, and Fidel is too sick to transfer."

"Flew them from Key West?" Pete asked.

Richard looked at the floor.

"They were already in Cuba. I'll fill you in on why later. They're in a small coastal city named Cardenas, taking care of Castro. Two nights ago a message between a Cuban major and a cartel boss was intercepted. There is an assassination planned for the near future. O'Malley wants you to phone him immediately."

He handed a yellow triangular Comsat phone to Richard.

"Quinn…Richard here."

"Team Mongoose being assembled, Richard. I have a special assignment for you."

"Yes, sir."

"My plane will be arriving at Big Bay in thirty minutes. It will get you here in an hour."

"How? Sending a fighter, Quinn?"

"My new plane does Mach 2. You'll like it. See you soon. Bring your suitcase." Quinn paused, just for an instant, then continued, "Tell the guys up there that their prayers would be appreciated."

Richard handed the phone back to Vincent.

"Need a ride to the airport. Quinn has a plane coming for me. And he asked that everybody pray for them. I've never heard him say a thing like that or heard that tone in his voice."

***

Doug squeezed down the hall and yanked a drunken couple, making love, from the phone booth. The young man, about to exhibit his manhood in front of the young lady, stepped back when he saw the look in Doug's eyes.

Doug closed the door.

…I need to get a cell phone…

"Honey, we need you at the bar to lead a prayer meeting."

"I'll be right there."

***

Getting through the throng packed into the old building proved difficult, even for Timothy.

"Machete, let me borrow Little Miss. Better yet, you lead the way to the bar."

"Chief, lend me your pistol."

"Machete," Chief Strait replied.

"A blind man waving a pistol, following a growling dog. Just picture it, Chief."

"BLIND MAN WITH GUN COMING THROUGH!" Machete yelled above the din. Suddenly the only sound was the pop popping from the popcorn machine and Little Miss growling.

"Holy shit, Chief, take the gun away from him!" shouted a patron backing away.

"I gave it to him, Randy, now get back."

Struggling and pushing, Timothy made it to the bar. Wendell and Wayne helped as he climbed on a chair and then stood on the counter.

"I apologize for interrupting your Friday night festivities," he said, looking down at the stunned people. "A dear friend has asked for our prayers this evening to help in a very difficult situation. Pastor Kate will be here momentarily to lead us in prayer. Those of you who are inclined are welcome to stay. Poor Joe's is closed."

"Whozzz schick?" someone asked, looking up at Timothy.

"We have friends who need our help," Timothy replied. The crowd opened a path, watching Pastor Katherine Kennedy McGinnis walk through.

She looked at her husband. Doug and The Usual Suspects surrounded her. Vincent whispered to her for at least a minute, and then the men lifted her to stand next to Timothy.

Holding Timothy's hand, Kate took a deep breath.

"Most of the time, in our day-to-day endeavors, we feel as if we are at least partly in charge. Then the phone rings, or the hospital calls, or we get a report from our doctor, or a friend calls with a message of agony, and we realize we really aren't in charge of much, except for the love we can share and that we can together ask our Lord for His help and His guidance. And, sometimes we just realize we are helpless, that there is nothing we can do except to ask for a miracle. That is why we're gathered here tonight in this place, to pray and ask for a miracle."

Kate bowed her head.

Everyone in the bar bowed heads.

"Lord, we come to you tonight from this place many would find surprising to ask for your help. Our dear friends are in danger. We ask that you protect them. We ask that you help them defeat the evil ones just as you helped Gideon defeat a mighty enemy using his tiny army. We ask this in Jesus' name. Please help us."

Chapter Thirty-Five

Three Rare Human Beings

A yellow Mercedes 500 Taxicab, made heavier with armor plating and a twelve-cylinder diesel turbocharged engine, roared toward Colon, disregarding all speed limits.

"RICHARD, GET CHLOE!" Danielle screamed.

"Chloe is safe. She'll meet us in Colon."

"How? She's scared to death." Danielle began to cry.

"Actually, she's thrilled with her new phone."

"What?"

"She was studying, waiting for Stanley after you left, when the two agents assigned to her detail arrived and knocked on the door. Her bodyguard refused to open it more than the security chain would allow, peeking out. Chloe shouted in Spanish they had to wait until her daddy came home and added he would be home any minute. One agent slipped a Comsat phone through the crack after contacting O'Malley and told Chloe to talk to Uncle Quinn. With Chloe on the phone, Quinn handed the phone to Stanley. She opened the door and said, 'Let's go. You guys know Spanish?'"

"Oh my God. Will this day ever end?"

Thirty minutes later, the Mercedes pulled into a garage behind a three story blue, concrete building in downtown Colon. Richard pulled the garage door shut. Debra led and Richard followed Danielle up the stairs to the third level apartment, their weapons drawn.

"Mommy! Mommy!" Chloe yelled. "I won the race. Our team beat your team here!"

Richard laughed.

"See what Uncle Quinn gave me. It's one of those world phones like Daddy has."

"That's one cool phone, honey. You'll have to show me how to use it."

"Can't right now. Uncle Quinn said the lines would be busy for the next little while, and he would call me."

A young lady wearing a pink summer dress walked into the living room from the kitchen.

"Lunch is ready," she said in broken English. "Puerco asado…and yellow rice."

"Is it my imagination, or do you and Richard know each other?" Danielle asked across the kitchen table.

Richard looked up from his plate of Cuban pork and winked.

"You don't miss much, do you, Danielle? We met during an investigation in Alaska, where I was stationed."

Danielle put her fork down.

"Where were you stationed?"

"Anchorage."

The three adults in the kitchen looked at each other as the guards that transported Chloe looked through the windows in the living room.

"I think we should talk about it, Debra. My old boyfriend, Steven Chase, lived in Anchorage. The son-of-a-bitch tried to kill my husband. Is that the investigation we are talking about? Richard, are we talking about Steven Chase?"

"Yes, Danielle."

"Why were you there?"

"OK, here it is; here's the story," Debra said, looking at the hazel eyes that seemed to be staring right into her soul.

"Your old boyfriend is a major drug distributer for the Mexican cartel, under the guise of being in the oil pipeline maintenance business. He disappeared somewhere in Canada after he tried to kill Stanley, and then resurfaced in Key West, riding in a car with two of the top dogs in the cartel. And you guys fled to Cuba. I am the D.E.A. special agent in charge of the Anchorage district. That entails foreclosure and auction of all drug-related properties. Mr. Chase has a wife and three young children. Your pastor, Katherine Kennedy McGinnis, learned about the plight of Belvia Chase and her children, from Quinn. They were evicted. I'd rented a motel room for them. Kate flew up in Quinn's plane to help. Richard was on the plane, too. And, that's how I met Quinn and Richard."

Debra took a deep breath and studied Danielle's face.

"She took them home with her, didn't she?"

"Yes, they're in Big Bay."

"You may find this surprising, Deb, but I'm eager to meet her and her children."

"I'm not surprised at all, Danielle."

"You're rare human beings, you and Kate…very rare."

Danielle glanced at Richard who looked quickly out the window.

"A D.E.A. agent who rents motel rooms for a family after evicting them. Wow."

Chapter Thirty-Six

David Beat Goliath

Stanley sat on the brown, metal folding chair next to Quinn.

"I really thought I'd seen it all," Stanley said, looking at the black revolver in his hand. He spun the chamber twice. "Got that wrong."

He spun the revolver chamber again.

"Six bullets will not be enough, probably," he continued, looking at Quinn.

Quinn replied, "If we need more than six, Stan, it won't matter."

Fidel Castro pealed the sticky cardiac monitoring patches from his chest and climbed out of bed, triggering a piercing alarm. Doctor Gonzalez stood and turned the monitor off.

Then Fidel sat next to Stanley.

"These chairs are cold on a bare bottom!"

He looked at Stanley's revolver.

"My gun is shinier than yours," he said, bumping Stanley with his shoulder.

"That's 'cuz you're the president."

Fidel Castro looked at the blank monitor next to his bed. "Everyone in this room knows the truth. Living is the great challenge, my friends. Death is easy. You know personally, Quinn, as do I. You know Stanley.

Marco, you have seen this many times. We have seen the other side, my amigos. If today is our day to die, I can think of no greater honor than to travel with my good friends."

***

They sat quietly, listening.

Around midnight, Dr. Gonzalez said, "I'm worried about the rest of the staff and the patients here."

"I am too, Marco," Quinn replied. He removed the yellow Comsat phone from his jacket pocket, pushed a red button located on the top, and placed it on the bedside table.

"Just listen, men, while the best do what they do."

The phone remained silent until 1:30 a.m.

"Mongoose one…Armored personnel carrier exited garage at 13th Avenue and Obispo. Estimate: one-five-zero…that is one fifty, following on foot; twenty with RPGs (rocket propelled grenades)."

"Blackbird one in flight."

"Blackbird two in flight."

"Cantina…open for business."

"Uncle Sam on location. Ready to party."

Fidel looked at Quinn who put a finger to his lips.

"Maintenance man on duty."

"Mongoose six…Turkish anti-aircraft missile launcher at José Marti and Industria. Estimate one…zero…zero… That is one hundred. Following on foot. Three surface to air launchers."

"Sounds like they're bringing a tank to a gun fight," Doctor Gonzalez said sardonically.

"Got to give Major Prieto credit, Doctor; he's anticipating a battle."

"From the four of us?"

Fidel laughed.

Stanley spun the chamber of the black pistol again and took a deep breath.

"This is not the first attempt, Marco, but you know," Quinn said. "That's how you met, cutting a bullet out of him. There have been well-planned surprise attempts defeated. It seems the Major knows history."

"Mongoose seven…small battalion size…army regulars led by a youngster standing in an open jeep…directly west…one block…will be at location imminently."

Quinn picked up the transceiver and pushed the black button on the side.

"Await intentions of battalion. On my word, Robin Hood."

KNOCK…KNOCK…KNOCK.

Quinn walked to the door and opened it. Nurse Rhea, terrified, pointed towards the lobby window.

Two hundred young, Cuban army soldiers stood at attention, three deep, completely blocking the entrance and streets leading to Hospital de Cardenas. A young man in his early twenties stood facing the soldiers lined in front of him. He appeared to be speaking intensely, standing on the hood of a green Jeep.

"Fidel, you need to see this," Quinn said. "You truly need to see this, my friend."

The Big Bad Wolf and Robin Hood stood side by side, looking out at the young soldiers. Fidel's buttocks peeked through the open patient gown.

"I am going out to meet these brave men. Help me, Quinn, my legs are weak, and I need help with this IV pole thing."

Stanley, Rhea, and Dr. Gonzalez watched Quinn hold Fidel's arm and push the IV pole while a man in a soiled Caribbean Soul tee shirt pushed open the glass front doors. They walked side-by-side with Fidel's patient gown flapping in the gentle breeze.

"Mongoose one…Big Bad Wolf and Robin Hood on the street."

The young corporal stopped talking and stiffly saluted as Fidel and Quinn walked in his direction, IV bottles jangling against the metal pole.

Fidel returned the salute. The young man jumped from the hood. Fidel hugged the young soldier, whose head came to his shoulder.

"You remind me of my young self; what is your name, Corporal?" Fidel asked, looking at the soldier's insignia.

"Juan Castro, Mr. President."

Fidel smiled, listening to the engine sounds of approaching heavy military vehicles. He turned and faced the troops.

"You are very brave young men, and I salute each of you. I feel as if I am in the mountains again."

He paused and listened.

"I want right now for all of you to go inside. Join me in the hospital and watch what is about to happen to the enemy. Hurry. Inside. Everyone, there is room."

Fidel and Quinn led the young soldiers inside.

"Mongoose five…APC one block."

"Mongoose eleven…Missile launcher two blocks."

"Black Bird One is ready to eat."

"Black Bird Two is hungry."

"Robin Hood…stand by, Black Birds…counting down for a special gift from the President of the United States."

The black supersonic Stealth fighter flew low, fired one rocket, incinerating the Turkish missile launcher, banked tightly, and, flying fifty feet above the ground, fired a rocket at the armored personnel carrier, sending the gun turret spinning down the street and shrapnel into the troops following. And then it was gone into the dark night.

Fidel stared at Quinn who shrugged.

"Robin Hood to the Black Birds, you may feed."

The startled Mexicans and Cuban assassins regrouped and attacked the hospital from the north and the west.

Fidel refused to leave the front window, standing next to Quinn and the young corporal.

"What the hell, let's go watch," Stanley said to Marco.

"Watch and learn, Corporal. You are in for a promotion when this battle is won."

The darkness around Hospital de Cardenas suddenly disappeared in a brilliant white light. From their underbellies, the two strange-shaped flying machines unleashed hellfire from their Gatling cannons. Snipers lying on the surrounding rooftops stopped assassins running towards the hospital.

Fidel now had his arm on the young corporal's shoulder.

"Are you understanding how this is done?"

"I am trying, Mr. President."

"I will introduce you to the general who planned this victory," he said, nodding towards Quinn, "when this is all over."

Rhea slipped her arm around Stanley, standing next to Quinn, watching.

"You are very brave, standing here in danger, Stanley."

"I thought you couldn't speak English, Rhea."

"Spanish is sexier."

"That's what my daughter says."

"I hope Major Stupid is in that personnel carrier," Doctor Gonzalez said to no one in particular.

***

"Enough excitement, Mr. President, for one day; and seeing as we are alive, let's get you hooked back up to the monitor," Stanley said in the crowded lobby.

Fidel looked at Doctor Gonzales.

"You have dodged a bullet, so to say, and this is only day four…back to bed."

"No tent."

"Deal," Marco Gonzalez said. "Whew, I think maybe you have now seen it all, Stanley."

"Hope so. I'm looking forward to meeting my grandchildren someday."

"I'm looking forward to that day, too, Stanley, and having a little rum at your Poor Joe's." Fidel said, climbing into bed.

"Sinus Rhythm," Stanley said, looking at the cardiac monitor.

"I like a good battle," Castro said, looking at the monitor. "Sorry, you don't get to shock me."

He looked at Corporal Juan Castro, standing alone in the corner with a bewildered expression, and motioned with his hand for Juan to approach the bed.

"It has been a number of years since I had a chief of staff. I would like you to accept this position. You will be in charge of security and my daily schedule."

The young man seemed stunned and unable to fetch the appropriate answer. Finally, he said, "I am honored, Mr. President."

"Who are the troops you were addressing?"

"Battalion Matanzas. About half of us deserted Major Prieto when he disclosed plans to overthrow the government," the young man paused, "and the plans to assassinate you, Mr. President."

"That was very brave. You all could have been executed for desertion, you know."

"It is the right thing we did, Mr. President. The right thing is never wrong, regardless of the consequences."

"How old are you?" Dr. Gonzales interjected.

"Twenty-two."

"You are now the youngest general in the history of Cuba, Juan Castro—a general with bravery and wisdom beyond his years. I am honored to have you as my chief."

"I am the honored one, Mr. President."

"When you address your troops in the morning, General, advise them they are now the Presidential Guard."

"Never had one of those," Fidel said, winking at Quinn.

***

The yellow phone vibrated and a little red light flashed rapidly on the coffee table.

Chloe sprung from an overstuffed armchair.

"Mommy, it's Uncle Quinn," she said, looking at the identification screen.

"Hi, Chloe, how are you and your mom doing in Colon?"

"Kinda boring, Uncle Quinn."

"I bet it is, honey. Here's your daddy with good news."

"Hi, Chloe, want to come back to Cardenas?"

"I like that hotel not as much as Uncle Fidel's house. I miss my classes."

"We'll talk. Put Mom on the phone."

Stanley listened to Danielle breathe into the phone.

Chloe, Richard, and Debra watched the tears overwhelm Danielle's eyes and trickle down both cheeks.

"The bad guys are gone, honey. It's over. We're fine, we're all ok."

"I have been so scared and saying prayers all the time. Laid on the couch last night and tried to remember the sound of your breathing and prayed I would hear it again."

Chloe stared at her mother, watching her trembling lips move.

"Wait a couple of days, and then you guys come back."

"Can't come back now?"

"You wouldn't believe the mess outside, honey. And we really don't want Chloe to see it."

He listened to his wife breathing.

"It was like some sort of miracle, Danielle."

"David beat Goliath," she whispered.

Chapter Thirty-Seven

A Genuine Miracle

Poor Joe's remained closed following the prayer meeting. It became the sentinel location, awaiting word from Cuba. The doors remained open on Saturday for inquiring patrons, but no alcohol was served. Dora prepared large platters of free cold-cut sandwiches, and the popcorn popper popped constantly. But, no alcohol, and Timothy remained firm despite objections.

"Wish I was down there," Timothy said glumly.

Chief of Police Strait stared into the Goebel Beer mirror behind the bottles of liquor. "If we had known, I think we all would have been on our way, too," he said to the men sitting around the long poker table.

"The hard part," Wendell said, "is wondering."

...spitting gritty, bloody dust...like catching a fly ball...Timothy leaning against the 50 Cal...screaming something...damn grenade...

"Wondering what?" Machete asked from the south end of the table. "Wondering what, Wendell?"

"I guess if they're still alive."

Timothy slammed his fist on the table hard enough to cause the full cups of coffee to spill a little.

"Damn it!" he said, looking at the man who had saved his life in Vietnam.

Machete stroked Little Miss faster than usual.

...a party...Wendell carried Chloe...her eyes told me...just touch her...Maria...can't burn this Poor Joe's...

Vincent Bonifacio fiddled with his yellow ComStat phone, spinning it on the table.

Doctor McCaferty poured creamer into his coffee cup until it overflowed and sent a little stream towards Machete. Little Miss lapped at the beverage dripping from the end of the table.

Doctor Varner looked at Timothy and shrugged.

Pete walked to the popcorn machine and turned it off for no particular reason.

"Damn it, me too, Wendell, and I feel ashamed of my weakness. I can't imagine life without them."

Dora watched Doctor Lavern Smith walk through the front door with a tired face, still wearing his white coat. From the kitchen, she watched the men she admired and sipped a coffee cup filled with potato vodka and one ice cube.

***

Katherine Kennedy McGinnis stood and opened the big Bible on the podium to First Corinthians.

She glanced at the first row of pews, looking at her husband, their son, and Tiffany's three children.

A little uncomfortable away from the familiar surroundings of their Immaculate Conception Church, Doctor Smith and his wife sat next to Wendell in the second row.

Belvia Chase and her three children sat on the other side of Wendell. Rose and Ralph sat next to Belvia's youngest. Rose held five year old Edmond's hand.

...thank you, Lord for this life and opportunity to share your love...

"And now these three remain," Kate recited, looking into the filled sanctuary, "faith, hope and love. But, the greatest of these is love."

"Why is love the greatest? Why did Saint Paul write that love is greater? I think that Paul was saying that without love, we have nothing."

"Jesus' very own brother, Saint James, wrote that faith without works is dead. I think Saint Paul was telling us that without love, faith is dead and there is no hope. Love is our foundation."

Vincent Bonifacio walked briskly through the open front doors of Big Bay Methodist Church. He walked down the center aisle without hesitation.

Kate spotted him as he approached and stopped speaking. Vincent climbed the steps to the podium and approached her. She extended her right hand to him and, when he grasped it, she pulled him closer. He bent down and whispered.

Timothy began to tremble. Carla moved even closer and held his hand. Wendell watched and then looked down at the hardwood floor. Dora started to cry.

Little Miss stood up and licked Machete's hand. Machete smiled.

"Last Friday night we had a prayer meeting at Poor Joe's," Kate said.

"We prayed for our friends. They were in great danger. I can now tell you that we were praying for Stanley, Danielle, Doctor Gonzalez, Quinn O'Malley, and for the patient they were caring for, Fidel Castro."

A distant siren's sound drifted through the open doors into the silent sanctuary.

Little Miss' tail thumped on the floor.

Heads twisted briefly towards the open entrance doors. A red and white ambulance wailed down the street.

"This is an associate of Captain O'Malley's. He just had a conversation with him. An assassination attempt has been thwarted. The evil ones are defeated. The Lord listened to our prayers. Quinn told Mr. Bonifacio it was nothing short of a miracle that they are still alive."

Kate clenched the podium with both hands.

"He listened to our prayers, and He helped us. Prayers work, my friends. We need to never forget, especially on our gray and cloudy days, when our waves of doubt are about to swamp our little boats, that our Father in heaven has not changed, that He loves us very much."

Carla watched her husband's shoulders slump forward, his head down.

…thank you, Jesus. I'm very sorry I doubted…I should know better…I'm sorry…

Little Miss dragged her harness on the hardwood floor. She stopped next to Timothy and licked the top of his head.

Chapter Thirty-Eight

A Pale Shade of Red

Juan Veracruz replaced twelve exhausted candles and lit the new tall ones, left to right.

"Uncle, I have heard nothing, maybe tonight."

He sat behind the great desk and turned the shortwave radio to the Monday-designated frequency.

"Point Man to Goaltender…Point Man to Goaltender."

He adjusted the antenna trim and fine-tuned the frequency before attempting again.

At three a.m., Juan extinguished the candles, right to left.

Staring at his family portraits hanging in the dim light, he said, "Maybe tomorrow we will hear from our soldiers or perhaps Major Prieto. I am sorry, Uncle."

***

Richard maneuvered the armored Mercedes around the destroyed personnel carrier and turned left towards Hospital de Cardenas. Debra sat in the front seat next to him with her service pistol on her lap. Danielle watched the carnage go by from the back seat. Chloe watched through the passenger side rear window.

"Looks like a war, Mom."

"Daddy and Uncle Quinn said the bad guys are all gone now."

Richard backed the car into the parking lot next to the hospital, the car pointing towards the street.

"My God, look at the hole above the cantina," Debra muttered to Richard.

"RPG. Damn, they had RPGs, Deb."

They turned left and faced the hospital.

"Holy shit!" exclaimed Chloe. "Look at the bullet holes."

"Language, Chloe." Danielle admonished.

"Daddy says it."

Richard laughed. "That he does, honey."

Danielle, holding Chloe's hand firmly, followed Richard and Debra, both with their sidearms in hand, walked closer and closer to the bullet-riddled concrete hospital.

"They're gonna need new windows," Chloe said. "And doors."

Twenty feet from the shattered doors, a young lady with long, blond hair emerged from the alley to the west and walked towards the group.

They stopped and watched her coming closer.

Richard studied her face. Debra glanced at her pale white hands.

"Can we help you?" Debra asked, taking several steps to block her from getting closer to Danielle and Chloe.

"I'm happy you made it back from Colon safely," the blond lady said in a voice reminiscent of the wind blowing gently. She placed her right hand on Debra's right shoulder and moved her aside without effort.

The touch felt warm, and Debra felt every bit of anxiety sucked through the blond lady's hand.

"Hi, Chloe."

"You were in my room…at the hospital!" Chloe said. She pulled away from Danielle and walked to her. "I remember you talking to Machete and Little Miss, when Machete promised something. Then you kissed me on the forehead before I woke up."

Richard took a deep breath.

Danielle and Debra moved closer.

"Hi, Janet Sue," Danielle said. "You were here with them, weren't you?"

The blond lady looked through glowing eyes.

"Yes. Danielle, your husband and your friends were being looked out for." She smiled. "That Quinn O'Malley is quite a general, though."

"I know you, don't I?" Debra said. "Kate and I know you."

"You will hear your husband breathe tonight." She turned back towards the alley and disappeared around the corner of the hospital.

"Holy shit!" Richard exclaimed.

"Language!" Chloe laughed.

"I know her," Debra said. She sat on the bench in front of the hospital, swatting at flies feeding on specks of blood. She looked up at Richard.

Chloe looked at her mother, shrugged, and grinned. "Told you, Mom."

"Let's go inside," Richard said, holding his hand towards Debra.

"This has been quite a week," he said, pulling the broken door open.

***

"Hi, Daddy!" Chloe shouted, while running towards his arms spread wide. "Richard drives faster than you do!" And she sprung upward.

Danielle joined the hug.

"Janet Sue met us outside, honey."

The room became very quiet, except for the soft beep-beeping coming from the cardiac monitor.

"Where?"

"Just before we walked in."

Quinn O'Malley rubbed his whiskers.

Doctor Gonzalez asked, "Who's Janet Sue?"

"You believe in angels, Doctor?" Richard asked.

"Yes."

"Good."

Fidel Castro pulled at the hairs on his left eyebrow.

"This has been the week from hell," Doctor Gonzalez spoke from a metal folding chair against the wall, his handsome face a map of fatigue. "One week ago you called me with pain between your shoulder blades, Mr. President, and an ache in your jaw."

His glazed, brown eyes looked up at Quinn and Stanley. "Thank you for being with me during this purgatory. The president and I would not have survived if not for your friendship."

He looked at Debra and Danielle. "The men you have chosen to be with are examples of true friendship, of a loyalty most never know. I am grateful."

"That's why I married him," Danielle replied. Moving closer to the doctor, she brushed his dark hair away from his forehead with a gentle caress. "Unconditional is the only thing he knows."

Debra took Quinn's callused hand in hers and said nothing.

"I have a medevac helicopter scheduled to arrive at 1400 hours. I'm flying Mr. President to Havana Hospital. It has been seven days since the MI, no further VT. They can do a cardiac catheterization and intervention, if needed. And, it is time to leave here. Thank you. You are dear friends. I am so thankful I met you in Key West at the wedding."

"The honor has been ours, Marco," Stanley said. "Our meeting was no accident."

"Please stay at the villa in Nueva Gerona and rest," Fidel Castro said, "for as long as you like."

"Oh boy!" Chloe exclaimed. "I love that house and the school."

"That makes me very happy, little one," Fidel Castro said.

***

At precisely 2 p.m. a blue helicopter with ***Hospital de Habana*** painted in bold white letters on the belly flew over the still smoldering armored personnel carrier and landed next to Hospital de Cardenas. Stanley, Danielle, Chloe, Richard, Quinn, and Debra watched from the sidewalk as Doctor Gonzales and the flight medics loaded Fidel Castro. Doctor Gonzales waved, and the door closed. The helicopter lifted and pointed west. It was joined by two green Russian- built helicopter gunships.

"Are those helicopters as good as the ones you have, Uncle Quinn?"

"They sure are, honey. Let's take a plane ride to the Isle of Youth. You drive us to the airport, and I'll get you home, Richard."

"If it's all the same, I'd rather stick around a while longer, Quinn, if you don't mind."

"We'd like that," Quinn answered.

They climbed into the big yellow Mercedes disguised as a taxi.

A warm rain began to fall. The little creeks flowing along the curbs in front of the hospital were soon a pale shade of red, flowing towards the ocean.

Chapter Thirty-Nine

The Precious Time

Stanley winced, grimaced, and twisted awkwardly, removing his shirt.

"Where'd you get that shirt? Danielle asked.

"Marco loaned it to me."

"What's wrong, honey?" Danielle asked, watching him struggle and then pulling on the shirtsleeve to help.

She saw the bandage wrapped around his right bicep.

"Marco does a great dressing, don't you think?"

"Why do you need a bandage, Stanley?"

"Kinda got caught up in the moment…standing too close to the window."

"DID YOU GET SHOT?"

"Kinda…clean in and out…didn't hit anything important."

"What am I going to do with you?"

"I've got several ideas."

"I just bet you do."

***

Quinn and Debra sat side-by-side in white wicker chairs on the balcony, looking down at the town and the water in the distance.

"I'm going to resign from the D.E.A."

"Why?"

"Too many scumbags. Time to be around some kind people."

"You gonna join the Peace Corps?"

"No. I see you've done your homework."

"What then?"

"I'm going to sell my place in Anchorage and move in with you."

Quinn stared at the horizon where the sun had just disappeared.

"I live on a boat, you know."

"Slip 8, right next to the Conch Republic Seafood Company. I've done my homework, too. The Key West Dreamer."

Quinn chuckled.

"I want us to be together, Quinn. I don't want to hear about the difference in our ages. I watched Timothy and Carla; they adore each other, and Kate and Doug. I asked Kate about the age difference. She giggled, Quinn. She giggled and said their love is better than anything she had imagined. I know that it's likely I will bury you, but the precious time we have together will eclipse the agony of losing you. Anyway, you'll be there waiting for me when it's my turn."

"Don't bury me. I want to be sprinkled off Mallory square."

"I want this more than anything I've ever wanted, Quinn."

Quinn turned, put both arms around Debra, and pulled her tight against him.

"You want me to ask Kate to marry us?" Quinn asked

"Already taken care of, honey."

Chapter Forty
One Yellow Envelope

Stanley swallowed two acetaminophen and codeine tablets, washing them down with a rum and coke, ten minutes before going to bed.

Danielle walked out of the shower with a towel wrapped around the top of her head and found him gently snoring. She smiled and lay down beside him in the darkness, listening to him breathe, her tears flowing freely down both cheeks and disappearing into the soft pillow.

He woke with a start the following morning, the sun shining on his face through the open window. Danielle's side felt warm and a little damp. He listened to the sizzling sounds coming from the frying pan in the kitchen and inhaled the smell of dark Cuban roast coffee.

A yellow envelope fell off his chest when Stanley rolled over. He opened it.

Dearest Stanley,

I was just sitting here thinking about you. I can hear you breathing in the bedroom. I lay beside you last night and listened, too. Pretty soon you will wake up and you'll be asking if I'd like some yogurt and would I like banana or strawberries on top.

I try really hard to let you know how much all of the small things you do for me every single day equal a big thing. Because of all you do for me to make my life more wonderful, I only ever smile when I think of you, and my heart warms...I get excited.

Most people grow tired of one another after just a few short years; I picked you because I knew my life would always be interesting with you in it.

Thank you for being everything I imagined you would be in my life. I know I would not be who I am today without you in it.

I am very proud of you, living life to the fullest and not wasting a minute. You're quite a guy.

You are the very best of the best, and I'm hopelessly in love with you.

FOREVER YOUR LOVER, DANIELLE

Stanley read the letter three times.

"Would you like bananas or strawberries on top today, honey?" he said, wrapping his arms around her from the back and kissing the back of her neck.

Danielle twisted her head around.

"I just want to go home."

"Me, too. Thanks for the love note."

"I mean every word. How's your arm?"

"It throbs."

"Seriously, I want to go home. I miss Big Bay."

"What about Steve Chase?"

Danielle twisted the rest of the way around in Stanley's embrace.

"I will meet with him if that's what it takes, honey. I'll tell him to get the hell out of our lives, that I never loved him and want him to go away."

"Or, we can have Richard shoot him."

"That would be easier."

***

"Point Man calling Goaltender...Point Man calling Goaltender."

Juan Veracruz adjusted several knobs while staring at the yellow dials.

"Point Man calling Goaltender."

He turned in his office chair.

"I am sorry, Uncle. Tomorrow I will send Jose Antunez to Cardenas and find the answers."

Chapter Forty-One

Two Black and White Glossies

Three friends walked alone on the long dock at the small marina in Nueva Gerona. "Arm hurt much?" Quinn asked.

"Not if I don't think about it," Stanley replied.

"That's the secret," Richard said. "I've had practice."

"I wanted us far away from any potential listening devices," Quinn continued. "Have news on two fronts. First, the cartel is sending a shipment by sub tomorrow, along with a hit man by the name of Jose Antunez. The new cartel boss, cousin of Jesus Veracruz, hasn't heard from Major Prieto or the men he sent to Cardenas. That's good news; means the vermin were eliminated. There wasn't much left to identify in either vehicle. We're tracking the sub."

The men stopped to admire a 1950's fishing trawler.

"How'd they get subs?" Stanley asked.

"Money and greedy Turkish naval commanders. Deb shared a classified secret."

"She'd be in trouble if that leaked out, Quinn," Richard said, scratching under the glass eye.

"She's quitting anyway…and that's classified," Quinn retorted.

"Second, we've been flying search patterns over the Gulf for the past week. Two nights ago, a scan found something at 12,000 feet. Had a shrimper send down a deep submergible with a camera."

Captain O'Malley removed two pictures from his shirt pocket, three inch by five inch black and white glossies. He handed them to Stanley.

"This is a crushed German sub, the type being used by the Mexican drug cartel. I believe this is how the cousins and Steve Chase escaped Key West."

Stanley and Richard stared at the two pictures.

"We can go home," Stanley said, looking at Richard.

"I want to be the one to tell Belvia," Richard said.

"What about the sub coming in?" Stanley asked.

"Cuban Special Forces are going to hit it with depth charges when it reaches shallow water."

Quinn smiled. "There's going to be plenty of white powder floating on the bay."

"Leaping euphoric dolphins coming for miles," Richard added, smiling his crooked smile.

"Debra said the D.E.A. is going to be really pissed."

"What can I tell Danielle?" Stanley asked Quinn.

"What do you usually tell her?"

"Everything."

"Now is not the time to change, Stanley."

***

"What you reading?" Stanley asked.

"*5 de Septiembre*," Danielle said from the wicker chair on the balcony, looking up from the newspaper.

"Really?"

"It's my assignment. Chloe has enrolled me in her Spanish class. I'm her first student."

"How's it going?"

"Better since she has written the English translation above each line."

"Good luck."

"You're next."

"I have the discs you bought me."

"I think you're already enrolled, and you haven't listened to a single lesson."

"We can go home, honey," Stanley said, sitting in the chair next to his wife.

He handed Danielle a black and white glossy picture.

"What's this?"

"Quinn's guys found a German sub lying on the bottom of the Gulf and a rubber dingy washed up on the coral reef offshore from Key West. The Mexican cartel has three of these subs. Quinn is confident that Steve Chase and the cartel cousins are in it. Quinn said below 500 feet the pressure would crush that sub. They are at 1,200 feet."

"Oh."

She held the picture and then looked over at her husband.

"Guess I won't have to tell him to go to hell."

"Or, enlist Richard's help."

She handed the picture to Stanley. "He tried to kill you...good riddance. Oh, Doctor Gonzalez called for you. I wrote his new number on the pad next to the phone.

***

"Hi, Marco, Danielle said you called."

"How's your arm?"

"I think I should be on an antibiotic."

"I'll bring you some amoxicillin."

"You coming here?"

"Have someone I want you to meet and to ask for a favor."

"Of course, Marco, you know that."

"I want you to meet my fiancé."

"I didn't know you were engaged."

"Asked her yesterday. After last week, it was time."

The conversation stopped for several seconds.

"I watched you marry Miriam Pico and Doctor Roosevelt, and Kate and Doug in Key West."

He paused.

"Would you marry Marciana and me?"

"I'd be honored. Would it be legal here?"

"President Castro will be a witness and sign the license."

Stanley laughed. That'll make it legal, Marco. How's Fidel?"

"Cathed day before yesterday…90% proximal right coronary artery…two stents. Ejection Fraction estimated at 80 percent. He's going to be fine. No other significant blockages."

"Wonderful!"

"Marciana and I will fly down tomorrow. I want you guys to meet her."

"Don't forget my amoxicillin."

"Just put it in my bag."

Stanley placed the black Bakelite phone receiver in the cradle. He turned to see Danielle standing in the entrance to the balcony, the bright sun shining through her short summer dress.

"Do you have any idea how damn sexy you are?"

"As long as I turn you on, mister."

"Marco is flying down tomorrow, bringing me some amoxicillin."

"He's flying all that way just to bring you antibiotics?"

"He wants us to meet his fiancé."

"Good for him. Never have understood why some gal hadn't reeled that handsome man in."

"He asked me to marry them. See what you got started."

"What's her name? Did he tell you?"

"Marciana."

"Marciana Gonzalez. Sounds like a movie star or rock star. I bet she's beautiful."

"Marco asked her to marry him. I bet she's an amazing human being," Stanley said.

"Then we go home, Stanley. After the wedding, we ask Quinn to fly us home."

"I wonder if we still have jobs."

"Who cares," Danielle said, rubbing against Stanley.

Chapter Forty-Two

Nearly Perfect

…hope they like me, she thought, climbing out of the helicopter…

"**L**ook at them!" Danielle exclaimed, watching Doctor Marco Gonzales and his fiancé walk away from the Cuban Air Force helicopter, which had just landed on the villa helipad. "She's so petite…and beautiful."

Debra and Quinn watched from the third floor balcony. Richard stood on the other side of Debra.

Marco's fingers hurt a little from Marciana's grip, squeezing him tightly with a sweaty hand. They walked up the slight incline towards Stanley, Danielle, and Chloe.

"They look as I imagined, Marco, the picture in my mind."

Marco replied while waving, "They epitomize love. You and Danielle will be close friends before you realize it."

"What does epitomize mean?"

Marco grinned. "They are examples of love."

Chloe ran down the incline and jumped, anticipating Doctor Gonzalez would catch her.

He did.

"Chloe McMillen, meet the lady who is going to be my wife," he said, lowering Chloe to the ground.

Marciana's dark eyes sparkled. She went to both knees on the grass, looking up into Chloe's curious hazel eyes.

"I am honored to meet you," Chloe said in Spanish.

"The honor is mine, Chloe. It is nice to meet you," Marciana replied in Spanish.

"Thank you. You are very beautiful," Chloe replied in nearly perfect Cuban dialect.

"I think you are beautiful, too. You look like your mother. I am very impressed by your Spanish."

"Thank you. I am teaching Mom Spanish. Not sure if Dad is ready."

"Perhaps you can help me improve my English someday."

"I sure will!" Chloe said.

Stanley and Danielle walked down the slope.

Danielle slipped on the wet grass and fell on her butt.

Marciana sprang to her feet like a cat and ran the few feet to Danielle. She put both hands out to help her up.

"It is nice I meet you, Danielle," Marciana said in broken English.

"The honor is mine, from the ground up." She grasped Marciana's hands and pulled herself up, looking back at the wet grass stain on her ivory dress.

"Here's your amoxicillin, Stanley. Want me to take a look at your arm?"

"Sure."

"Lina is preparing lunch," Danielle said. "I'm going to change and then we'll have a chance to talk."

"I need to wash my knees," Marciana said, looking down.

"Quinn and Debra are joining us and our friend Richard. Don't let Quinn scare you, Marciana."

"I have met Quinn, Stanley. He is the reason my Marco is alive today."

***

"Enchilada de Camarons!" (Shrimp Enchilados), Marciana exclaimed. "My favorite!"

"Mine, too," Debra said.

"And Lina makes the best ones I've ever had," Quinn added, piling several on his plate.

"How'd you two meet?" Debra asked, looking at Marco and Marciana sitting next to each other at the big round table.

"She was sitting in the hospital cafeteria all alone eating lunch. I walked past her to get in the buffet line, and, when I got to the cashier, she was walking out. I left my tray on a table with some interns and walked as fast as I could without embarrassing myself, to catch her. The elevator door opened, and I went in with her."

"He was like a little boy," Marciana interrupted, speaking slowly, searching for the correct English words. "He stood there looking at me, with not a word coming from his mouth. Even though it was only my third day at hospital, I knew who he was. All the ladies in the office want him; they say he is the smartest doctor on the staff. Everyone knows he is President Castro's personal physician. He looked at me and I put my hand towards him and said, 'Hi, my name is Marciana,' and he said his name is Marco, but I could hardly hear him say it. That is how we met."

Doctor Gonzalez's face grew progressively redder.

"Which hospital?" Stanley asked.

"Hospital Calvito Garcia in Havana," Marco replied, regaining his composure. "Marciana is the hospital's comptroller. She has a Ph.D. in normative economics."

"What ought to be," Stanley interjected.

Marciana's head jerked towards Stanley.

"That's correct, Stanley, from the ancient Greek...rules of the house. How did you know?"

"I read it somewhere, I guess."

Marco leaned close to his fiancé and whispered. She smiled at Stanley.

"Marco told me you married several of your friends in Key West. Would you marry us?"

"Yes. I am honored. Have you decided on a location?"

"We'd like it here at the villa, in two weeks," Marco said.

'This is a beautiful place to be married," Marciana said, "and to start our lives as one."

"Two weeks would be August first...a Saturday," Danielle said, looking at a calendar in her checkbook.

"That is perfect," Marciana said. "Is the weather nice in August where you live?"

"Nearly perfect," Stanley answered.

"Marco and I would like to honeymoon in your Big Bay."

Marciana reached out and touched Chloe's hand. "Would you be our ring bearer, holding our rings during the ceremony?"

"!Si!"

"I would like very much for you to be my best man, Quinn."

"Yes is the answer, Marco."

Danielle looked up from her plate to see Marciana staring, her head down slightly, brown eyes glistening.

The same fingers on his left hand tingled a prickling, cold pain, and Marco imagined they must be white; Marciana's tight grip under the table trembled, and her leg shook a little.

"I want you to be my matron of honor," Marciana said to Danielle without blinking.

Danielle stood, and then Marciana stood.

Stanley, Marco, Quinn, Richard, and nine-year-old Chloe watched as the two ladies embraced next to the window without saying a word.

"Thank you very much. We have to be back at the hospital day after tomorrow. We'll be back in two weeks!" Marco said.

From the kitchen, Lina watched.

Chapter Forty-Three

Like Spearing Fish in a Barrel

Lina turned the lights off in the villa kitchen at 10 p.m. She walked quickly to her apartment on the ground floor, entered, and locked the heavy wooden door. Pushing aside neatly folded pink panties in the middle dresser drawer; she removed a small Zenith shortwave transceiver.

Carefully, Lina unfolded a sheet of onionskin typewriter paper and placed it on her little desk. Reaching up, she turned the switch leading to an ultraviolet light hanging over the desk. The light revealed columns of letters and numbers.

"Great Chef to Point Man…Great Chef to Point Man."

"Point Man…ready to copy."

"18-15-2-9-12…break…8-15-15-4…break…1-12-9-22…break… 1-20…break…22-9-12-12-1…end. (Robin Hood alive at villa)

"2-9-7…break…214…break…22-15-12-6…break…1-12-9-22- 5…break…8-15-16-9-20-1-12…break…8-1-2-1-14-1…end. (Big Bad Wolf alive Hospital Havana)"

"Good copy, continue," Juan Veracruz replied. And he continued to transcribe the code of the day.

"Both at villa…1 August wedding."

"Security impenetrable. Will wait," Point Man replied in code.

"Possible group gathering of all in Big Bay, USA, mid- August. Will advise."

"Like spearing fish in a barrel. Advise with details. Out."

Juan Veracruz sat in the soft office chair, leaning forward, rubbing the dark stain in the wood of the large oak desk.

"This time, Uncle," he said without looking up. "This time I will avenge our family. They will soon regret their transgressions. I promise this, Uncle."

Lina pulled the light blue dress over her head and tossed it on the bed. The mirror fogged over as the water sprayed down from the showerhead. The hot water cascading over her head eased the tightness around her eyes and released the aching spasm in her neck.

...someday soon I will not have to share that man...

She cupped both hands, filling them, and splashed the warm water against her cheeks, remembering the warmth of Godfather's body when she pulled him close. The warm water made the burn on her right hand hurt where she had touched the cast iron pan while making flour tortes at lunchtime. Her neck began to tighten again, thinking of his blond wife.

Chapter Forty-Four

True Friends

"**T**he president is coming soon," the wrinkled old man smoking a cigar said to the young boy.

"How do you know?"

"The fighter jets…they always circle when he stays at the villa," the old man replied, pointing with his cigar at the circular contrails over the island.

The noise made by two C-130 Hercules turboprop planes, each accompanied by two Cuban helicopter gunships flying in the direction of the 8000 foot runway at Rafael Cabrera Mustelier Airport, caused people to run out of the buildings in Nueva Gerona for a look into the sky.

Both gigantic Hercules planes had *United States Air Force* printed on their fuselages.

"Perhaps Nueva Gerona is being invaded," the old man said.

"Yuppi!" (Yippee) the young boy said, waving his hat from the hilltop at the large planes.

Looking down from the second slow flying Hercules, the pilot saw the old man and little boy standing on the hilltop next to a grapefruit orchard and wagged the wings of his plane as he flew over.

The little boy jumped up and down with glee.

From the first Hercules, a T-54 tank exited and drove rapidly in the direction of the villa. A Cuban made BM-21 multiple rocket launcher and S-125 surface-to-air missile launcher followed the tank. When they were in position at the intersections leading to the hilltop villa, the great door to the second Hercules lowered.

An open 1959 Jeep drove down the ramp first, driven by General Juan Castro. Fidel Castro sat next to him, smiling. A large Cuban flag flew from a pole attached to the back bumper.

Following the green Jeep were three large rack trucks with 100 Presidential Guards in each.

"I want to drive through town first, General," President Castro said to his chief of staff.

Juan glanced at Fidel with a questioning look.

"Really," Fidel replied to the look.

At the intersection of Street 32 and Street 41, right in the middle of the roundabout, Fidel said, "Stop!" He climbed out of the Jeep and shook hands with two attendants from the Servi-Cupet gas station and then walked into the gathering crowd as Juan signaled to the soldiers in the first truck to disembark. He pushed through the crowd to be at his president's side, his hand on his sidearm.

Twenty minutes later, they were once again driving up the hill towards the villa.

"That is why this has all been worth the efforts," Fidel said.

"I about wet my pants," the young general said.

Fidel laughed, listening to the flag flapping behind them.

The wrinkled old man and little boy watched from the hilltop. Then the old man patted the top of the boy's head.

***

Quinn O'Malley walked away from the welcoming friends waiting at the landing pad, watching the convoy led by the open Jeep driving up the hill. He held Chloe's hand and walked towards the speeding vehicle with the flapping Cuban flag.

Everyone watched the two old friends embrace. Then Fidel picked up Chloe. She said something and kissed him on the cheek.

"He shouldn't be lifting like that," Stanley said to Marco.

"You tell him, Stan."

"He's lost weight," Danielle commented.

***

The six men sat on the balcony off the great round room, talking and gazing out towards the ocean.

"Mr. President, I have a favor to ask," Marco Gonzales said.

Fidel looked from face to face before he said, "Every man here has saved my life at one time or another. I would not be here if each of you had not helped me. I was thinking about this on the way up the hill after shaking hands and seeing the smiling faces in town. None of this would be happening if not for each of you. Quinn, from the early days. Remember that Sunday night, Quinn?" And he pointed down the hill at a large round gray building. "You lost a front tooth that night."

"Deb wants me to get it fixed," Quinn said.

"I know a good dentist," Fidel continued. "There would have been no revolution if not for that night; Batista was going to execute me. My 15-year sentence—truly a death sentence. And last month I was privileged to watch men of character do the right thing once again with little regard for safety. I owe you my life. There is nothing I will not do to help you. You are true friends."

He paused and looked up at the fighters circling and then down at the tank blocking the lone road leading up the hill.

"Going to be the safest wedding in all of recorded history." He shook his head. "What did you ask, Marco? I'm sorry."

"Marciana's father died when she was a child. She is an only child. Would you walk her down the aisle?"

Fidel answered, "Yes. I am honored. Her father died during a battle in the Sierra Maestra Mountains. I am honored to repay that debt."

"Marciana never told me," Marco said. "She'll be excited."

"She doesn't know you were going to ask?"

"I wasn't going to tell her you said no. She arrives tomorrow; I'll tell her in the morning."

Fidel looked from face to face again.

"I am serious. I am here for each of you, just as you have been there for me."

Lina looked at Stanley, Marco, Richard, Juan, Quinn, and Fidel sitting on the balcony. She watched from the great round room for several minutes before opening the door and saying, "Lunch is served downstairs."

"Tomorrow is going to be a glorious day," Marco said.

"It will be, indeed, Doctor. And I have a surprise-wedding gift. We're all flying in my plane to Big Bay next Thursday for a wedding reception being thrown by the kindest people you'll ever meet," Quinn said.

"You're unbelievable, Captain O'Malley," Marco said, shaking Quinn's hand.

"Well, your sweetheart said she wanted to honeymoon in Big Bay."

"Am I invited?" Fidel Castro asked.

"The man who gives the bride away is invited," Quinn said, nudging Fidel with his elbow. "It's all taken care of, my friend."

"By the way, how did you get the loan of those C-130s, Quinn?"

"I know a man who owed me."

Lina watched the group walk towards the elevator, talking and laughing.

Richard studied Lina's face right before the elevator door closed.

Lina noticed Richard staring at her.

...that glass eye is creepy...

Chapter Forty-Five

On the House

Judge Linsenmayer said to the assembled around the poker table, "The Gonzalez's may use my cottage on West Bay for their honeymoon. This is so exciting!"

"I don't think I've heard Stanley this excited for a long time," Timothy said from the other end of the long table, twirling a strange looking phone on the cherry wood.

"Where'd you get that thing?" Wayne asked, pointing at the phone.

"O'Malley gave it to me when he and Debra left for Key West."

"Can we have some popcorn?" eight-year-old Norah Chase asked Timothy.

Timothy smiled at Belvia.

"Mom said we have to ask."

"Yes, Norah. Thanks for asking. You guys may have popcorn anytime you want, on the house."

"What's that mean?"

"Free."

"It's free, Mom!"

Belvia Chase's lips formed "thank you" from the southwest table.

"The wedding is tomorrow at Castro's villa in Nueva Gerona. The doctor and his fiancé want to honeymoon here. His name is Marco—for those who didn't meet him at Kate and Doug's wedding in Key West. His fiancé's name is Marciana."

"Why was the doctor at Kate's wedding?" Belvia asked.

"He's Fidel Castro's personal physician."

The confused look intensified on Belvia's face.

Timothy laughed. "President Castro was meeting with our president at the Truman White House. That's where Kate and Doug were married by Stanley. Castro asked that Stanley be on his medical detail while in the country and that is how Stanley met Dr. Gonzales and they became friends. Actually, a lot of us in this room met Castro at his villa. He and Quinn negotiated a problem for us."

"You're rambling," Carla said, sitting next to Belvia. She leaned toward Belvia and said,

"The guys have had several occasions to meet Fidel Castro and Dr. Gonzalez. It's really exciting that the newlyweds want to be here for their honeymoon."

"It's going to be a mother of all parties," Pete exclaimed as he helped himself to another draft Schlitz.

"I called David Chown in Traverse City. He can make it. I left a message on the Roosevelt's answer machine in Carmel, inviting Miriam and Jim. Rose and Ralph are coming. Vincent Bonifacio said he's bringing a date."

"Jenifer down at Jen's Place is going to pitch in and help with the buffet," Dora said from the kitchen.

"There going to be Cuban food?" Wendell asked.

"Jenifer Gomez—her daddy is one of those boat people escaped Cuba on a raft—lives in Little Havana and owns a restaurant where Jen learned to cook."

"I take that as a yes," Wendell replied, rubbing his gray head.

"One week from tomorrow night, guys," Timothy said.

He paused and looked at all the people in his bar.

"In my wildest teenage dreams I could never have concocted a movie like this, guys. Wendell and I thought we were goners at the Saigon Embassy." He paused again and took a long gulp of beer, trying to wash down the tremor in his voice. "Who could have ever dreamed of this life?" He looked at Carla and his son, recalling the kidnapping by the Mexican cartel. "No matter the circumstance, we've been here for each other, because this is what friends do, no questions asked except how can we help. No judgments rendered. I am so thankful that I moved to Big Bay. Thank you for telling me about this bar, Wendell. And by the way, thanks for saving my life."

The bar became very quiet. Eight-year-old Charles Dwight Fife pushed, back from the table and walked to his father. He hugged his daddy without saying a word.

"Anyway," Timothy continued, his son hugging him, "our being here together at his time and place is no accident. I say we throw the MOTHER OF ALL PARTIES for our Cuban friends and start their journey as one with a beautiful celebration."

"I read about Fidel Castro in American History class," Charles said, looking up at his dad. "Is he coming?"

Timothy smiled and put a single finger to his lips.

"I think Jenifer Gomez hates Castro," Dora said quietly to Pete.

Chapter Forty-Six
Pure Adoration

"**I** feel like Cinderella," Marciana whispered, her arm through President Castro's left arm, looking up. Fidel looked down at her, entering the tunnel of swords.

Twelve Presidential Guards stood on either side of the garden path, wearing new blue uniforms, holding their swords high, the sharp tips touching in the bright morning sunshine.

Marco trembled, watching the lady with long dark hair, her eyes looking back at him with adoration, coming closer step by step.

"She's flat out beautiful," Quinn said, standing next to the groom.

Stanley watched Chloe walk a few yards ahead of Marciana and Fidel, carrying a satin pillow holding two golden rings.

…before we know it she'll be the bride… He looked at Danielle who was staring at her daughter.

"Who gives this lady to be wed?" Stanley asked.

"The president of Cuba is so honored."

Marciana hugged Fidel. "Thank you," she said, with her face against his chest.

Fidel sat on a folding chair next to his chief of staff, glancing up towards the helicopter in the distance, making concussive chop-chopping sounds in the air as it turned.

"People get married for all sorts of reasons," Stanley said. "They get married for cultural reasons, simply because it is expected, sometimes even arranged, sometimes to ease the awful agony of loneliness, or in hope of filling the holes in a broken heart and driving the awful gray feelings away. Sometimes people get married because of lust, sometimes because of love. Not that lust is wrong in a loving relationship; it's the thrilling, selfish ingredient that makes our hearts go pitter-patter. Love, on the other hand, is not selfish. Love is concerned for our partner's happiness. Love is a pure adoration for our partner, and that adoration will shine long after the lust has faded. When two people come together, lusting and loving, their souls are merged. Their lives are blended. They become one."

"When we watch you, Marciana, and you, Marco, it is easy to see that you desire nothing more than to be one, and we are very happy for you."

"Do you, Marco Gonzalez, take Marciana Rodriguez to be your wife?"

"I do."

"Do you, Marciana Rodriguez, take Marco Gonzalez to be your husband?"

"I do."

"Then by the power vested to me by the President of Cuba, I hereby proclaim to the world you are now man and wife. You came as two; you leave as one."

Marco placed a simple gold band on his wife's ring finger. Marciana placed a simple gold band on her husband's ring finger.

"Ladies and gentlemen and Mr. President, let me be the first to introduce the Doctors Gonzalez...husband and wife."

Fidel Castro raised his left hand slightly. The Presidential Guard came to attention and fired a seven-gun salute. As the newlyweds started down the tunnel of swords, five MiG 19 jets flew low in V formation over the wedding party, their engines idling so only the sound of the whistling wind over their wings could be heard.

"I do, too, Stanley James McMillen," Danielle said as they followed the newlyweds down the path.

Debra and Quinn held hands walking behind Stanley and Danielle.

"Let's do this, Quinn."

"Did you just propose to me?"

"I did."

"Yes."

***

Richard watched with amazement the big windows encircling the great conference room on the third floor, pulsating to the beat of a Cuban jazz band and the sound of laughter and chatter. Happy people, old college friends, a few family members, and colleagues from the hospital filled the room that, until this day, had been witness only to serious negotiations and military discussions around the huge round table.

Quinn watched Fidel who somehow assumed the role of bartender, squeezing limes and making mojitos.

…this is the most fun he's ever had…

"Would you like one?" Fidel asked, holding an ice filled glass with rum, crushed limes, mint, simple syrup, and bitters, topped off with club soda.

"I will, if you will."

The two old friends clinked their full glasses and took a sip.

"This is a beautiful occasion, amigo," Fidel said.

"Amazing where our paths have taken us, the people we have met," Quinn said, taking a second sip. "Look at these people enjoying life in this place simply because we met in college."

"I truly miss Dr. Blue, especially on occasions like this."

"I do, too, Fidel."

Marciana snuggled close to her husband, her chin against his shoulder, ignoring the silverware clinking against the wine glasses. Her dark eyes glistened with adoration.

"I am so happy I didn't settle," she whispered through the clatter.

Marco looked at her.

"I'm happy I waited for you," she continued.

"That makes two of us."

"How soon before we can leave?"

"I'll excuse us after the flan is served."

"I'm excited to be with you tonight."

"I'm happy we waited, Marciana."

Chapter Forty-Seven

Marie Lives There

At 10 p.m. Lina pushed the elevator button for the ground floor. She walked in the darkness to her room and unlocked the heavy wooden door, locking it after entering.

With petite fingers, she pulled open the middle drawer of the dresser. On top of the perfectly folded pink panties lay a white sheet of paper with a series of numbers, handwritten:

12-9-14-1 / 23-9-11-11 / 14-15-20 / 1-12-12-15 23 / 25-15-21 / 20-15 / 8-21-18-20 / 13-25 / 6-18-9-5-14-4-19

Every place on her body tingled with fear. Frantically, she pushed the panties aside and retrieved the Zenith radio and code sheet.

Spreading the code sheet open on her desk under the ultraviolet light, Lina transcribed…

Lina I will not allow you to hurt my friends

Slowly she turned. The blue light illuminated Richard's glass eye with a cold hue.

"Do you understand," Richard asked in perfect Cuban Spanish, "that you and your lover will never be allowed to hurt my friends?"

Lina trembled.

"How did you know?" she asked. "How did you know the code?"

"The code is simple. I memorized it the first time I listened to you on the shortwave."

Lina let out a long shaky sigh.

"You are not a mean, evil person; I know mean and evil when I see it. I understand the reason you are involved, Lina. Love can be a tough slave master. You are being used."

"What now?" Lina asked.

Richard pointed in the direction of the transceiver.

"Call Juan Veracruz," Richard replied, glancing at the clock on the wall. The hands pointed to ten-thirteen.

"Great Chef to Point Man…Great Chef calling Point Man."

Juan Veracruz adjusted the antenna trim slightly to the left and replied.

"Point Man here. Proceed with report."

Richard gently took the microphone away from Lina.

"Worst Nightmare to Point Man."

"Repeat."

"This is your worst nightmare speaking, Juan Veracruz."

Nothing but static for several seconds, then weaker signals of voices fading in and out before Juan replied.

"Do me the honor of identifying yourself, nightmare man."

"My parents named me Richard Elmore Fortin."

"You speak with a Cuban accent, Richard Elmore Fortin. How can I help you?"

"I'm from Iowa. Your girlfriend has a message she wants to read," Richard replied, pointing to the note on the desk.

The typewriter paper trembled in Lina's hands. Richard held the microphone to her lips and she read, "Lina, I will not allow you to hurt my friends."

"You are a brave man, Richard Elmore Fortin, when you are dealing with weak women. I would like to meet you in person. It will be a short visit."

"I am looking forward to that meeting as well. You will not fare well, Juan; this I promise."

"You talk brave in the presence of women. We will see."

"That is my point; you will not see. I will arrive like a jaguar during a foggy, dark night. One moment you will be thinking about your evil enterprises; and the next instant you will be answering to God Almighty."

Lina sat on the bed, weeping.

"Richard Elmore Fortin, you are a dead man."

"We are all dead men, Juan. I have died before. You will not hurt my friends; this, I promise you."

The static on the radio in Lina's apartment was not interrupted by Juan Veracruz. Richard turned the radio off and sat on the bed next to Lina.

"Juan will send someone to hurt me, won't he?'

"He is a mean and selfish man."

Richard reached into his pants pocket. He placed an amber colored plastic bottle with a white cap on the bedside table. Lina opened it.

"Red capsules?"

"Seconal. They will help you sleep."

"Perhaps I will sleep forever."

"The music has colors there, Lina."

"How do you know?"

"I have visited, where the music has colors. My sister Marie lives there now."

"I will say hi to Marie for you."

Richard stood up and, bending over, kissed Lina on the top of her black-haired head.

"That glass eye of yours is scary, Richard Elmore Fortin."

"I know."

Chapter Forty-Eight
In Spanish and English

They were partway up the hill towards the grapefruit orchard when the wrinkled old man and little boy looked up towards the western roar. The young boy removed his hat and waved.

"It has the roar of seven planes," the old man said. He lit a cigar, which the boy had rolled earlier, after breakfast.

"I have never seen an airplane like that one, Uncle."

"Nor have I, little one. These are mysterious days."

They stood in the warm morning sunlight, watching the sleek white jet with a needle nose disappear towards the north.

"How fast did you say this goes?" Fidel asked Quinn.

"Fifteen hundred miles per hour. We'll make Big Bay in a little over an hour."

"You remember the first time—the time we took a biplane for a joy ride—I asked you if you'd ever flown one and you said, 'How hard can it be?'"

"The bravery of youth, Fidel. We lived and you led a revolution."

"The bravery of youth," Castro replied, gazing from their table towards the front of the plane.

Richard, Juan Castro, Fidel, and Quinn sat at a table in the back of the Gulfstream S-21, Fidel and Quinn facing towards the cabin. Stanley and Danielle sat at a table with Debra. Debra faced towards the tail of the plane.

The newlyweds rested in leather recliners in the prone position, side by side, holding hands. Chloe laid in the third recliner next to Marciana with a smile on her nine year old face. Six members of the Presidential Guard occupied the remaining seats.

"Quinn looks worried to me," Debra said, looking past Stanley to the men talking at their table.

"We've lost track of Juan Veracruz," Quinn said. "The guys babysitting him, say his armored Mercedes is in his garage. The front gates have remained closed, but it is obvious now he isn't there. Somehow he slipped out two nights ago."

Fidel rested his chin on his left hand, his forefinger rubbing his left ear. "Well, shit," he muttered.

"Quinn, you want me to fly back to Mexico City and look for him?" Richard asked.

Young General Juan Castro's eyes widened with a confused look.

"No, Richard," Fidel answered as Quinn thought. "That is his playground and he will have the advantage. Better he comes to your playground."

"I wanted to keep this away from Big Bay," Quinn interjected.

Fidel Castro shrugged.

"But," Quinn continued," you are once again correct, my friend...the bastards never stop trying to hit us. Since the meeting with Raul Veracruz and his grandson, Cesar, in your villa those many years ago, the cartel has planned to even the score."

Richard rubbed under his glass eye and wiped away some drainage before he spoke. "I promised Juan Veracruz he was not going to hurt my friends."

Fidel smiled. "You will keep that promise."

Debra watched the men talk. Quinn looked up and saw her stare and winked.

Danielle watched Debra's eyes.

"List the possible ways they can enter the city," Fidel said.

"Three highways: one from the west, one from the south, and the Seven Hills Highway from the north," Quinn replied. "And then there is the airport, the bus depot, the river, and the bay."

The young general reached into his briefcase and withdrew a map. He unfolded it on the table.

"I had this delivered to me when I realized my president was going to Big Bay."

The men at the table looked at a detailed map of Big Bay County, including a city street map of Big Bay. The general had drawn a red circle around the location of Poor Joe's. At key intersections leading into the city and at a boat launch below the dam, as well as the airport and Greyhound Bus Station, there were little red X's.

"I am only remiss in knowing where the president is staying while in Big Bay. The assassins must never reach here." And he pointed to the circle around Poor Joe's. "These are the locations where we wait and stop them dead should they travel that direction," he continued, pointing at the X's. "We do need more men," he said, nodding at the six Presidential Guards sitting in the front of the plane.

"Damn, I can pick them, can't I, Quinn?" Fidel said, looking at his twenty-two year old chief of staff.

"He's staying at our place."

Everyone looked up from the map at Stanley, who was looking over Richard's shoulder.

Stanley leaned in and pointed to the address on the bluffs overlooking the city.

"We've got a concern, Stanley," Quinn said.

"Did you know that Debra could read lips, Quinn?"

"I guess I do now, huh?"

"In both Spanish and English."

"I should have known."

Fidel reached up and gripped Stanley's hand. "Tell the ladies at your table we have all eventualities anticipated, and that no one will be interrupting the celebrations in Big Bay. I have been looking forward to Poor Joe's for many years."

He paused and looked at the reclined couple holding hands.

"And the newlyweds are going to have a glorious celebration."

Stanley smiled and squeezed President Castro's hand. "That's exactly what I am going to tell them."

"I have three helicopters flying in; actually will arrive prior to our arrival. That will give us thirty-six men for starters," Quinn said.

Richard smiled his crooked smile. "Juan Veracruz has no idea who he is dealing with."

"And a Secret Service detail is in Big Bay right now. They were sent to provide additional protection, Fidel."

"I'm happy he won a second term," Fidel said. "We talk nearly every month since our meeting in Key West. He would like me to visit the White House in Washington before he retires…or before I die," he said with a grin.

Quinn punched a series of numbers followed by the letter V on his yellow telephone. He spoke to Vincent Bonifacio for several minutes, concluding with, "Thanks, my friend. See you tomorrow."

He put the phone back in his shirt pocket and looked at his friend since college.

"Our friend from St Paul has connections with the Italian business community. There is no love lost when it comes to the Mexican drug cartel. Vincent is chartering a plane to fly fifty businessmen from his community to help in any way possible, as long as I can find someplace for them to stay. Told him not a problem, between the hotel and homes that will welcome them…as soon as I let Timothy know what's going on."

"Think you can coordinate all this?" Fidel asked his young general.

"Yes, sir. Absolutely, sir."

"They have a plan and we're going to have a party," Debra said, watching the young general fold his map and place it back in the briefcase.

She looked at Danielle's worried eyes.

"With these guys looking out for us, I'm not worried in the slightest, Danielle; I've been around."

Danielle smiled a little smile. "If you're ok, me too. I've just seen all the evil I ever care to see."

Debra took a deep breath and simply answered, "Yup."

Chapter Forty-Nine
It Goes Without Saying

Chief of Police Larry Strait sat at one end of the long poker table. Timothy Fife sat at the other end. Wendell, Pete, Wayne, and Morris sat at the west side of the table. Machete with Little Miss sat on the east side with Ralph and two city cops, and Doug. Dora fussed about in the kitchen and then decided to bake peanut butter cookies for the men.

The *CLOSED* sign faced towards the street, hanging from the screen door spindles.

Timothy breathed out a long sigh. Pete, sitting closest to Timothy, saw his eyes glisten.

"There is going to be a party here on Saturday night, a wonderful celebration." He twirled the yellow telephone like a top on the cherry wood.

"I spoke to Quinn on this phone ten minutes ago. The plane with the newlyweds, Richard, Stanley, Danielle, and Debra will be here in less than an hour. That's the good news."

"What's the bad news, then?" Morris asked.

"The Mexican cartel has put a hit out on some of us—those who were in Cuba nine years ago during the negotiations with the cartel godfather—specifically meaning Chief Strait, Wendell, Quinn, Stanley, and myself. We would just be the frosting on their cake. They're really after Quinn and Fidel Castro, and I guess Richard too. Quinn said Richard has really pissed off the new godfather."

Chief Strait rubbed at the tightness on his forehead while he spoke. "Are you saying Fidel Castro is on the plane with the newlyweds?"

"He is, along with his chief of staff and six body guards."

Machete lifted his head from a bowed position and turned his face slowly in the direction of each person around the table.

"I don't know what to say, I guess," Machete said in a soft voice. "It seems that evil never rests." He rubbed his blind eyes. "I have visited where there is no evil, where I could see the color of music, so I do not fear death. You station Little Miss and me at the front door, Timothy, and I promise no evil will enter."

Timothy stood and walked to Machete. "I love you, you crazy little Mexican," he said, rubbing the top of Machete's head.

…*A true miracle*…Timothy thought as his fingers felt the indented scar from the bullet wound.

At the same time, Pete and Wayne said they would guard the back door.

"Here's the thing, guys. We cannot have a gunfight like when the Hells Spawn bikers trashed Norma's party, not with our guests here."

Timothy walked around the bar, aimlessly while talking.

"Quinn said three of his Stealth helicopters will be flying in shortly with thirty-six True Believers. The US Secret Service is going to provide protection for Castro."

"And," he said with a little smile, "Vincent Bonifacio, who, by the way, is coming with his girlfriend, is flying fifty Italian businessmen here to, as he put it, help in any way possible. I've already found them places to stay.

"We will all meet here tonight, 1900 hours, to map out a defense should the assassins show up and to guarantee our visiting friends from Cuba a wonderful time."

"It goes without saying," the former Green Beret lieutenant colonel concluded, "that this information will not leave the room. We're going to have the mother of all parties; that's all our loved ones need to know."

Doug stood, looking up at the clock above the bar. "Let's get our wives and meet the plane when it lands."

"Great idea," Chief Strait said.

"Cookies are out of the oven," Dora announced. "The ones on the right have chocolate chips in them."

"You come too, Dora; bring Machete."

"I'll drive," Machete said, looking in the direction of the kitchen.

Chapter Fifty

Home!

Richard smiled, looking out the window.

On approach to the Big Bay Regional Airport, the Gulfstream S-21 had slowed to two hundred miles per hour. As it turned for the final approach, a Stealth helicopter rose alongside and flew fifty yards off the starboard wing.

Richard tapped Fidel Castro on the shoulder and pointed.

"It is a beautiful machine," Fidel said. "You miss flying them, I am sure."

"Terribly."

Danielle looked down at the approaching airport.

"Oh look, a welcoming committee!"

From the descending airplane, the occupants saw a cluster of people near the private hanger next to the Big Bay terminal. Two Stealth helicopters idled on the ground, ready to lift-off at a moment's notice. A black Suburban idled between the helicopters with four men wearing sunglasses standing next to it.

From the ground, the crowd looked in amazement at the sleek, white plane with a pointed needle nose while it circled once, a Stealth flying machine by its side. Then the helicopter lifted to the right, and the plane landed.

Stanley peered through the window, watching a reception line form. He smiled, watching Dora lead Machete. They stood in a line: Machete and Little Miss, Dora, Timothy, Carla, Katherine, Doug and their son Charley, along with Tiffany's three children, Belvia Chase and her three children, Wendell, Morris, Pete, Wayne, Jenifer from the diner, Rose and her husband, (a former member of the Poor Joe's' Usual Suspects) who had just arrived from Las Vegas, Chief of Police Larry Strait, and his wife Dawn.

Opposite the hometown welcome line stood seven True Believers, dressed completely in black, facing the hometown folks.

Doctor McCaferty, Doctor Varner, Doctor Fox and Doctor Smith arrived, with their wives, riding in Doctor McCaferty's rusty yellow Suburban.

Timothy smiled as the rattling vehicle stopped in the parking lot.

...Jack loves that old truck...Old Yeller...

Quinn walked from the back of the plane to Danielle. He pointed.

"See the lady—seventh in line wearing the teal dress—with the three kids?

"Yes, I don't recognize her."

"That's Belvia Chase."

Danielle sucked a short breath in and stared.

"She's a beautiful lady," Danielle said.

"Danielle, she doesn't know her husband is dead."

"You want me to tell her?"

"Richard will."

"Then I'm just going to hug her."

Two Secret Service agents pushed a ramp with metal steps and bulletproof Plexiglas, to the plane. They trotted up the steps. From inside, the door opened.

"This is your homecoming," Fidel Castro said from the back of the plane. "You go first, please. And hug your friends. I will be along shortly."

Chloe bounded off the plane and down the steps. She kissed Machete, hugged Little Miss. She stopped walking down the reception line in front of the Chase children.

"Hi, my name is Chloe, what's yours?"

"I'm Norah."

"I'm Miranda."

"I'm Edmond."

"Where do you live?" Chloe asked.

"In the big house next to the Methodist Church's preacher," Miranda said.

"I'm happy to meet you. I'm going to give Spanish classes. Would you like to learn?"

"Yes!" all three answered.

"What's Spanish?" Edmond asked after Chloe walked down the line.

Belvia smiled.

"You're going to be amazed when Fidel comes out," Timothy said to Carla. "He will remember the name of every person he met during the Key West wedding."

"He will not. Bet he doesn't remember me; only met him for five minutes at the Truman White House."

"Bet's on. What do I win?"

Carla winked at her husband.

Richard disembarked from the plane next. Belvia left the line and they embraced, silently.

Stanley and Danielle walked down the metal steps together to the applause and cheers of the assembled. The True Believers clapped, too.

Timothy and Stanley hugged. "Damn happy to see you home, buddy," Timothy said.

"I have stories for poker night," Stanley said with a grin.

Stanley and Danielle turned and faced the ramp. Stanley walked to the ramp as Marco and Marciana started down.

"Everybody, I want you to meet the newlyweds. Meet Marco and Marciana Gonzales"

Even louder applause erupted and a few whistles from The Usual Suspects.

Richard looked past Belvia's shoulder and relaxed his squeeze. Gently he turned Belvia around and hugged her from behind.

Danielle extended her hand to Belvia.

"I am Danielle McMillen. It's nice to meet you."

Belvia took her hand and then asked, "May I hug you?"

Danielle squeezed Belvia's hand and pulled her close, embracing her.

Wendell watched from his spot in the line. "They look like they could be sisters, don't you think?" he said to Pete.

Then President Fidel Castro walked through the plane door and stood on the landing to the astonishment of the reception line, except for The Usual Suspects.

"Your dog is beautiful, Machete; what is her name?"

"Little Miss."

"I was distraught when I learned of your shooting. I said a prayer, my amigo."

"It is my pleasure to meet you, Dora. I recognize you from pictures. I am looking forward to your cinnamon rolls this Sunday."

Dora gulped.

Timothy and Fidel simply hugged without saying a thing.

"I have your latest album, Carla. Your voice is fabulous."

He reached down and shook their son's hand.

"I am happy to see you," he said while shaking hands with each of The Usual Suspects, calling them by name.

"Hello, Dawn. Your husband told me years ago of your beauty; he was not exaggerating." Then he shook Larry Strait's hand and chuckled,

"You didn't think I would remember, did you?"

Jenifer Gomez stared at the old man walking down the reception line towards her, remembering the stories told by her father of escaping communist Cuba and nearly drowning when the little boat capsized in a storm, clinging to the rudder for three days before washing up on the Dry Tortugas.

…I can't do this…

She turned to leave the reception line.

"I am sorry if I have offended you," Fidel said gently, "or your family."

Jenifer Gomez turned back and faced him.

…oh shit…what do I say…

"I'm sorry, Mr. Castro. My father fled Cuba before I was born. He has told me stories about the awful things you did," she blurted.

The reception line grew silent. Two Secret Service men moved to get between Castro and Jenifer.

Quinn nodded to the True Believers.

Fidel Castro pushed one of the Secret Service agents aside and faced Jenifer.

"I am very sorry this happened to your father. What is your name?"

She hesitated before replying, "Jenifer Louise Gomez."

"There are many things, Jenifer, in our Revolution that I am not proud of, things in my youth that I am sorry for. I am truly sorry your father felt it necessary to leave the homeland."

He hesitated and looked at Quinn.

"You know this Quinn O'Malley?" he asked, pointing in Quinn's direction.

"Very well."

"He is my best friend. Would you please ride with us to your destination? I want to listen to your stories."

"My car is here."

"Tell Quinn where to have it delivered."

"OK, Mr. President."

The astounded watched as the Secret Service opened the doors to the black Suburban. President Castro climbed in along with Quinn O'Malley, Juan Castro, and Jenifer Gomez.

"I love this town, already," Fidel said to Quinn.

"Ok, I win." Timothy said to Carla.

"Yes you did," Carla said. She winked.

"Where're they headed?" Stanley asked one of the Secret Service agents.

"Your place," the man wearing dark glasses replied.

"You want my keys?"

"Not necessary…thank you."

Chapter Fifty-One

Lucky Seven

"Faith, I'd like you to meet Marco and Marciana Gonzales," Stanley said. "Marco is President Castro's personal physician. Marciana works at Hospital Calvito Garcia. She is the comptroller."

"I'm delighted to meet you."

"Faith is our circuit judge," Stanley continued. "She'd like you to use her vacation cottage on the beach for your honeymoon."

"I'll drive you down right now if you like," Faith said, watching two Presidential Guards carry suitcases from the plane. "I hope they give you some privacy."

***

Faith drove the lovers along the bay with the windows in her silver BMW open.

"This smells crisp and clean; the water is so clear," Marciana said from the back seat.

"This is fresh water," Faith said. "You could dip a cup in the bay and drink it."

"Oh, this is beautiful!" Marciana exclaimed when Faith steered the car into the cottage driveway and stopped.

...*thank you, Stanley*...Marco thought. He hugged his wife.

Faith opened the refrigerator door. "I tried to anticipate everything you'd need to get started," she said. "There's a little gas station grocery store half a mile down the road. You ok with a manual transmission?"

"I love shifting gears," Marciana said.

Faith tossed a set of keys to Marciana and opened the side door to the garage.

The honeymooners stared through the door at a polished, black Porsche 911 turbo.

"My summer car. Have fun, guys. It'll come in handy, too, if you need a little private time," she said, watching the Presidential Guard soldiers unloading suitcases from the trunk of an Oldsmobile.

"And," she said, smiling, "I'm the traffic judge. Just be careful, ok?"

The newlyweds went across the road after Faith left. They walked down the beach towards downtown in the distance and back, hand in hand. Marciana scooped a handful of water and tasted it.

Two soldiers walked about one hundred yards behind them.

"That Porsche is going to be fun," Marciana said, glancing back at the men. "Their Oldsmobile doesn't stand a chance."

Marco smiled and skipped a smooth flat stone on the calm fresh water.

"Seven," he counted. "That's good luck."

Chapter Fifty-Two

Seven Hills Highway

"**I** hate bats," muttered Juan Veracruz out loud to himself. Black winged mammals fluttered from the tunnel ceiling and darted at the yellow light coming from his flashlight. He walked, bent over, through the tiny tunnel leading from the basement in his house to the city storm sewer system.

...hope they're not vampire bats...

Yesterday he had called a cousin working at the Mexican Embassy in Washington D.C.

"I need diplomatic papers and credentials," he demanded. "I need a limousine with diplomatic plates."

"Why?" she asked.

"You know better than to ask."

"OK, when?"

"Friday. I'll call when we are in D.C."

He stepped out of the escape tunnel for the first time into the large, dark storm sewer. Both eyes watered; uric stench and the odor of digested refried beans caused him to gag. The brown water sloshed on his shins. The paving bricks were uneven and slippery. His right leg bumped something. In the dim illumination, he looked down at a head with matted hair and sunken eyes, bobbing away.

For six blocks, Juan walked through the sewer system under Mexico City, shining the dim flashlight at the ceiling, looking at the numbers above each connecting drain. At number 66 he turned right and crawled through a small tunnel. When he reached the end, he lay on his back and pushed up with his legs against a rusty, metal trap door.

"You need a shower," a fat man said, helping Juan through the opening in the liquor store floor. Juan looked at his watch and nodded. "Clean clothes, please."

***

Four Secret Service agents stood alongside their Suburban—two on either side, straddling the center line of the eastern highway leading into Big Bay—bright little blue and red lights flashing from inside the grill, its taillights flashing in an alternate fashion and the headlights flashing from low to high beam rapidly.

"This will not be a problem," the driver in the black Cadillac stretch limousine said, coming to a stop with the headlights of the Suburban flashing in his face.

"Shoot them if we have to," Juan Veracruz said from the front passenger seat to six men behind him.

One Secret Service agent looked briefly at the diplomatic plate on the front of the car. A second agent walked to the rear, shining a flashlight at the license plate with a diplomatic tag and said something in his radio.

The first agent tapped on the driver's window.

It opened and the driver said, "This is Carlos Jose Flores, Ambassador of Mexico to the United States. We are en route to Big Bay at the special invitation of the President of Cuba for a reception he is holding for his recently married friend."

The limo driver spoke without hesitation and without blinking, staring at the agent glaring through the open window.

The six men in the rear of the limo leaned against the doors, awaiting the indication to spring out and shoot.

The agent standing at the rear of the limo had a discussion on his portable radio. Then, he said something to the agent next to the limo driver about the license plate being registered to the Mexican Embassy.

"Sorry for your inconvenience, Mister Ambassador. Have a wonderful time at the reception."

***

Miriam Roosevelt had just finished singing *Besame Mucho* to the honeymooners, first in Spanish and then in English, ending with the verse,

"Kiss me more, kiss me many more times as if this beautiful night is the very last time."

Little Miss began growling before the Cadillac limo appeared in the light of the street lamps, driving slowly down Union Street with its headlights off.

Machete reached up from his chair and held her collar.

"Evil is coming near," he said to Richard, standing next to him on the sidewalk in front of Poor Joe's. One of the two Secret Service agents standing alongside the front steps said something in his wrist microphone.

Richard said, "They are here," into his yellow telephone and handed it to Machete.

David Chown began a piano solo following Miriam's set, playing Fidel Castro's favorite Chopin works, starting with the *Revolutionary Clavier.*

Wall-to-wall people packed the century-old bar well beyond the occupancy rating.

Marco and Marciana sat next to each other at the long poker table heaped with wrapped gifts and surrounded by happy strangers welcoming them to Big Bay.

"I think I could live here, honey," Marciana said.

"Their love is real, no doubt about that. Quinn was telling the truth."

Fidel Castro sat at a little round table next to the piano with Dora, Debra, and Quinn.

Juan Castro and several Presidential Guards sat close by.

"What time do you start baking the cinnamon rolls in the morning?" Fidel asked Dora.

"Seven, so they have time to cool before I frost them. Why?"

"I'll be here at seven. Brought some special Cuban coffee beans with me. I'll make us café con leche while the rolls are baking. You have a coffee grinder?"

Dora smiled and shrugged a little, pointing to the grinder next to an old espresso machine.

Kate, Danielle, Belvia, and Carla sat at the big round table in the southwest corner with their six children. Stanley, Doug, and Timothy worked behind the bar making mojitos.

Fidel turned his head, watching a young lady with long, blond hair walk down the stairs. The crowd seemed somehow to part for her, and she moved through them. She walked past him, stopping just briefly to touch him on the shoulder and to smile. Then she proceeded to the southwest table and sat next to Danielle who began to tremble. Kate bowed her head.

...be with us Lord...please protect us...

The limo stopped directly in front of Poor Joe's.

Both Secret Service agents held automatic rifles at the ready.

Richard walked to the limo and tapped on the driver's window. It came down, and he looked in.

"Ambassador of Mexico to the United States, Carlos Jose Flores, here at the invitation of the President of Cuba," the driver said.

Richard bent down and looked past the driver towards the

passenger. Then he walked around the front of the limo and tapped on the passenger side window.

In Spanish, he said, "Juan Veracruz! I am your worst nightmare. Finally we meet, face-to-face, as you wished."

Juan shook his head. "How does a farm boy from Iowa have a Cuban accent? Amazing."

The six men wearing full body armor waited tensely to leap from the limo, their machine guns ready.

Richard pointed in the direction of a dark alley off Union Street. The street lamp at the intersection was not lit.

"One of the True Believers has a rocket propelled grenade targeted on this vehicle as we speak. A second RPG is aimed at you from the rear."

He paused.

"The blind man sitting on the steps is the man who shot your cousin, Jesus, whose blood still stains the floor just inside the entrance," Richard said pointing. "I think he is some sort of spirit with awesome powers."

Richard paused with his head cocked a little to the right. "If you listen carefully, that is the sound of an amazing flying machine with a Gatling cannon that will reduce this vehicle to shreds in an instant."

"You will die, too," Juan said with sarcasm.

Richard smiled. "I know."

Both the driver's side and passenger side windows rolled up. The black Cadillac stretch limo drove away. It turned left on Front Street and followed the street to the Seven Hills Highway then turned left, driving north.

Twenty Italian businessmen standing in the darkness around Poor Joe's lowered their assault rifles.

Richard ran up the steps into Poor Joe's and waved to Quinn. Outside, they conversed for several seconds before Quinn spoke into his yellow transceiver.

"Location of limo?" he asked the navigator onboard the helicopter.

"Approaching bottom of first hill, the Seven Hills Highway."

" Mongoose team one," he radioed to the True Believer roadblock one mile from town, "let the limo pass. Just disappear."

"Ten-Four, Robin Hood."

The Limo had just crested the seventh hill when the Gatling cannon turned it to scrap metal. The Stealth flying machine banked tightly and fired an experimental uranium-nitrogen-magnesium incendiary rocket, reducing the Cadillac to a brilliantly burning molten blob.

The blond lady, her shining eyes twinkling, stood up and briefly touched Danielle's hand.

"Who was that?" Belvia asked. "She never said a word."

Kate, Danielle, and Carla said, almost at the same time, "You'll get to know her."

She walked past Fidel Castro. He looked at her face. "You should marry the lady," she said in perfect Cuban Spanish.

*...her lips never moved...*Fidel felt the exciting prickles exactly like that moment he entered Havana.

He stared at Dora.

Janet Sue walked up the stairs, stopping just long enough to wink at Wendell.

"Let's have a girl's night before Miriam flies back to Carmel," Danielle said.

Carla said, "I remember the afternoon you guys dragged me out of the house when I came home from Mexico City. You made sure I was over served!"

"I really can't afford it right now," Belvia said.

"My treat, Belvia," Danielle replied.

"You know, you two could be sisters," Carla said, looking at Belvia and Danielle.

"We know. Kinda sick, don't you think?" Belvia replied.

Chapter Fifty-Three

Nearly World Famous Cinnamon Rolls

The lights were not on, except for in the kitchen, when Fidel Castro walked up the steps and a Secret Service agent opened the unlocked door.

"I didn't really think you'd show up," Dora said, watching Fidel walk towards her with a slight limp.

"You've been on my mind all night."

"Short night."

"Sleep is overrated; nothing a good cup of con leche won't fix."

Dora laughed. "You're a tough old man."

Fidel dumped a pound of dark roasted coffee beans, filling the glass container above the grinder, and pushed the start button.

"Rolls will be out in fifteen minutes. I'll make some cream cheese frosting," Dora said, walking to the refrigerator.

"I'd like one hot out of the oven, with butter."

"Me too!" Dora said. "I don't like cream cheese frosting, but the guys love it."

The two friends sat at the little table next to the oven in the kitchen, waiting for the timer to ring.

"Ever been married, Dora?"

"Not even once," she replied, looking at the gray bearded old man.

"I'm determined not to settle for anything other than love, and it hasn't happened yet. How 'bout you?"

"I've settled for less than love many times. Married twice and many mistresses; you are the wise one, Dora, when it comes to matters of the heart."

"Fidel, answer me this; have you ever been happy, truly happy?"

"No, not truly happy; I think I would like to be. What about you, Dora?"

"I'm content seeing my friends and working here. I really don't want a broken heart. Seen too many broken-hearted people sitting at the bar. That saying about better to have loved and lost than to have never loved at all is a bucket of crap, Fidel. I've seen what a broken heart can do to a person."

"How can you be sure?"

"What?"

"How can you be sure it is love?"

"Ever been in love?"

"It appears not, by my track record. Just hoping each time, I guess," he said, picking up a hot cinnamon roll, dipping the edge in a bowl of butter, watching the butter melt.

"You're going to burn your mouth," Dora said. She stood, walked to the cutting block, and sifted powdered sugar into a bowl with a glob of room temperature cream cheese in the bottom.

"Quinn asked me to move to Key West a few years ago and live on his boat."

Fidel looked at Dora.

"We sat right there, at that table in the corner. He held my hand and I said to him that I'm not on this earth for his entertainment or any man's. I told him I truly treasure his friendship, and that I wouldn't consider anything that might damage our friendship."

Fidel put the cinnamon roll down and stared at her.

"You didn't come here after three hours sleep to help me frost cinnamon rolls. We feel something special when we are near each other. I saw it coming from your eyes when we met at the airport…and last night," Dora said, stirring the frosting.

She poured a tablespoon of vanilla into the frosting and a little half and half.

"You're a communist. I'm a capitalist. I don't understand how communism makes life better. You're an atheist. I'm a Christian. I love Jesus very much. I am a cook in a century old bar. You are the president of Cuba…get my drift?"

Fidel walked to Dora.

"I love the people of my country. I truly believed that communism would make their lives better after years of the corrupt Batista. As a young man, I dreamed of utopia. As a wiser old man, I know that corruption is not limited to capitalism, that greed is a human condition without boundaries. I am a socialist now, Dora. I believe we are here to help each other and to share with each other. Capitalism works. Communism does not."

Dora stopped mid-stir, leaving the mixing spoon in the frosting bowl, and faced Fidel.

"I have grown to appreciate Jesus Christ," Fidel continued. "I believe he is who he said he was. Actually, he has become my hero. I look forward to meeting him."

Timothy walked through the front door and turned the bar lights on.

Dora pulled the stirring spoon from the frosting bowel and pointed it towards Fidel's lips.

"Want a lick?"

Fidel tasted her special cream cheese frosting and smiled.

***

"That was a short night," Stanley said, standing next to Danielle in the kitchen, pouring boiling water into the French press.

"That coffee smells delicious."

"Fidel gave us a pound of his favorite beans. The Secret Service fellow on the porch told me Fidel left for Poor Joe's at seven this morning."

"Really!"

"Something about helping Dora frost the cinnamon rolls."

"Oh, brother," Danielle exclaimed.

"What?"

"Didn't you watch them last night?"

"Too busy," Stanley said.

"They were wooing each other like high school kids," Danielle said with a smile.

"Want to go down for breakfast?"

"I'm exhausted."

"Dora's soon-to-be-world-famous cinnamon rolls frosted by Fidel."

"Bring me one."

"Give you a ride in the Avanti."

"Bring me one. This is the best coffee I've ever tasted!"

***

She smiled when the familiar roar of the old Studebaker Avanti came from the garage and, as the sound became fainter traveling down the twisting road towards the city.

…he's probably going to take Castro for a ride…

Stanley tuned the car radio to News-Talk 580 and listened to the morning news by Joel Frank.

***

The first platter of frosted cinnamon rolls was half gone when Stanley walked in.

"Frosted by President Castro!" Wendell said, reaching for his third.

"Save two for Danielle," Stanley said to Dora who had just opened the oven door.

"Hey," he said to the men sitting around the table with their coffee cups, "did you hear the news this morning? A Meteorite crashed north of town last night…on the Seven Hills Highway?"

Quinn lifted the Sunday edition of the *Big Bay Recorder,* showing Stanley the front-page headlines.

METEORITE CRASH CLOSES SEVEN HILLS HIGHWAY. TEN FOOT CRATER SAID TO BE MILDLY RADIOACTIVE

"Damn, glad it didn't land in town," Richard said.

"We had one hit in the suburbs of Santiago de Cuba a few years ago. All that was left of a cigar factory was the sign out front," Fidel said, sitting between Quinn and Richard.

"Wonder how long the highway is going to be closed?" Pete said from the other side of the table.

"We had to fill the crater with concrete to contain the radioactivity," Fidel said.

"Yup, a lot of concrete," Quinn said. He handed the paper to Stanley.

Chapter Fifty-Four

Girls Night Out

"**W**e're having a girls night tomorrow night," Danielle said to Dora on the phone. I'll pick you up at seven."

"I don't leave until nine on Mondays."

"Except for tomorrow. Timothy will understand. What's he going to do, fire you? Just make a big pot of chili and they can help themselves."

"Thanks, Danielle; who's joining us?"

"Kate, Miriam, Belvia, Faith, Debra, and Carla. Going to Benjamin's Seafood."

***

Richard and Belvia were sitting in the booth furthest from the front door at Jen's Cuban Diner when the newlyweds walked in. Jen greeted them in Spanish with a big smile, hugging them both before seating them under a poster of old Havana.

"They sure look happy," Belvia said.

"I'm happy for them."

"I've never felt as happy as they look," Belvia continued.

"It probably helps to be in love," Richard replied.

"Good point."

Richard straightened the silverware around his plate and then reversed the fork and knife.

"What are you struggling to tell me?"

"Your husband is dead."

***

Danielle reserved a large table next to the deck railing outside at Benjamin's Seafood Company high atop Wayne Hill and overlooking the city lights far below. Gas heaters vanquished the little evening chill.

"Anyone want something other than the white wine I ordered?" Danielle asked, holding a bottle of Boskydel Vignoles. "Ben has it shipped in because Stan and I love it."

"Never had that," Dora and Debra said.

"Let's get the corks pulled and commence the festivities," Carla said.

Platters of stuffed crabs, calamari, and shrimp cocktail were served as appetizers.

"Jess, three bottles are not going to be nearly enough."

The waitress smiled at Danielle.

"How are things in Carmel?" Faith asked Miriam.

Mariam smiled. "Jim just bought into the big cardiology practice. I'm about half finished with my next album, and we have an offer on a house…used to be Clint Eastwood's." Then she smiled a very big smile. "And I'm expecting. Due in April."

"That's why you're drinking club soda!" Debra said.

"I couldn't be happier," Miriam replied.

"Sure glad you can be here with us," Kate said to Dora. "Timothy give you a hard time?"

"He gave me a hug and a fifty and said, 'Have a ball.'"

"We always do!" Kate said, pouring a second glass of wine. "This is the very table where Miriam and I made our wedding plans and we found out that Stanley could marry us."

"He was not a happy man when I let that secret leak out, but a good time was had by all," Danielle said. "And, just think, if we hadn't all gone to Key West, the honeymooners wouldn't be enjoying Big Bay at this very moment."

"How long are Marco and Marciana going to be here?" asked Dora.

"Marciana said two weeks, and then they have to be back at the hospital."

"Rumor has it that Fidel showed up to help you frost your cinnamon rolls Sunday morning, Dora," Faith said.

"He likes butter on his, hot out of the oven," Dora replied, looking at her plate. Then she looked up and saw everyone staring at her. "He wants me to go back to Cuba with him."

"WHAT!"

"When we are in sight of each other, it feels like a strong magnet, pulling us closer and closer. And, in the three days I've known him, my heart feels kinda gray when I'm not with him, and I think about him all the time. I feel like a teenager."

The ladies sat silently for several minutes, picking at the appetizers.

"I'd do it," Kate said. "At first blush, getting together with Doug was the craziest thing I had ever done. Look at us now. The best decision I ever made."

"Quinn and I are going to get married," Debra said, smiling at Kate.

Dora's head turned quickly towards Debra.

"Same magnet, Dora. I know the feeling. You guys are the first I've told."

"Wow!" Miriam said. "I need to fly back more often."

Kate looked at Belvia and noticed tears in her eyes. She reached under the table and held her hand. It trembled.

Danielle noticed. "What, Belvia?"

"I had lunch with Richard yesterday. He told me my husband is dead in a cartel submarine lying on the bottom of the Gulf of Mexico."

Debra took a deep breath.

"Telling the children is going to be the hardest. He was always kind to them."

Entrées of grilled grouper, whitefish and yellowfin tuna came to the table, served family style with yellow rice and spicy tatter tots.

"Richard has offered us his place in Key West; said he's hardly ever there anymore, unless we want him to be."

"You want him, don't you?" Kate asked.

"I think so; it's too soon, but I think so. I'm going to take him up on his offer."

"Well, Pastor Katherine, if you don't have a passport, I suggest you get one."

Kate looked at Debra.

"I've been to one wedding at Castro's villa. It is a beautiful place for weddings."

At eleven, a long stretch Lincoln limousine pulled into the parking lot below Benjamin's Seafood Company. Benjamin had checked on the ladies fifteen minutes earlier, asking if they enjoyed their meals. He counted the empty wine bottles and called the cab company.

...note to self...order more Vignoles in the morning...

The laughing ladies helped each other down the long wooden stairway towards the parking lot.

"Oh, I forgot to pay," Danielle said, part way down the stairs.

"I put tonight on Stanley's tab," Benjamin called from the top.

They all laughed.

*...I love these ladies...*Miriam thought, climbing into the limo.

Chapter Fifty-Five

A Radioactive Meteorite

At age thirty-three, Pablo Veracruz became the youngest godfather in Mexican drug cartel history. His cousin, the family counselor, and six elite soldiers had disappeared a month earlier while on a mission in the States. He assumed power on the sixth of September with minimal resistance, that resistance having been dispatched quietly. On the tenth of September, Pablo invited the heads of the five Mexican cartel families to the Veracruz compound for a summit meeting.

The summit meeting started on September fifteenth.

Pablo sat behind the big, shiny desk in the office with his family portraits on the wall to his left. Five family heads sat in overstuffed leather chairs, facing the desk, in a semicircle.

Outside, Mexican special police guarded the walled compound. Armored vehicles purchased from surplus U.S. military by the Mexico City Police Department, blocked the four streets leading to the compound, machine guns at the ready.

"We have lost two of our three submarines," Pablo said, opening the summit. "We have lost our distribution centers at Anchorage, at Saint Paul, Minnesota, at Las Vegas, at Havana, and Port au Prince."

"We have lost battles in Honduras, Cuba, Costa Rica, Panama, and most recently, in the States. We have lost our best soldiers," he continued, rubbing the dark stain embedded in the oak. "We have lost our great leaders, one after another."

"I beg your pardon, Godfather, perhaps they were not such great leaders after all; they lost, and they are dead," the head from the Cortez family said.

"It is obvious we cannot beat them with guns, Godfather. They have more guns, a Navy, and Air Force. We cannot compete on their level," Michal Chaves added from his chair under the family portraits.

Pablo listened to comments and debate for two hours. At noon he said, "I agree, we cannot win a war with guns. I believe we must buy our friends and share our bounty to re-establish our networks. Tomorrow morning we will formulate a new plan. I have entertainment arriving and delicious food being prepared here at this safe place."

***

It made almost no sound as it sped down the San Antonio de Banus Airfield, thirty miles southwest of Havana, only a whooshing sound. When the boomerang-shaped plane reached the altitude of forty thousand feet, it accelerated to Mach 4 in the direction of Mexico City.

Thirty minutes later the Stealth flying wing circled Mexico City. It slowed from slightly over three thousand miles per hour to four hundred.

Richard peered at the computer screen from his navigator's seat between the pilot and copilot. He ran a final global positioning check.

"Perfect." He grinned. "Wind co-ordinates active. Ready, sir."

Circling at forty thousand feet, the invisible flying wing launched one GPS-guided bomb.

At precisely 3:30 in the morning of September 16, the heavily guarded compound belonging to the Veracruz family for five generations exploded.

Burning a brilliant bluish-white flame, the entire compound

disappeared into a deep crater.

"I have kept my promise," Richard said to the pilot and copilot.

"The wing temp remained within acceptable range at Mach 4," he continued.

"Let's try Mach 5 on the way back," the pilot said, turning the plane east and nudging the throttle forward. Two neutron thrusters responded immediately.

Richard Elmore Fortin smiled his crooked smile.

Mexico City's newspaper, *Aristegui Noticias*, ran this headline in the paper's Monday morning edition...

METEORITO DESTRUYE COMPUESTO RADIACTIVO FAMILIA VERACRUZ

Chapter Fifty-Six
Seems Surreal

They stood barefoot, side-by-side on their condo deck, wearing only Turkish bathrobes—white, with the Cuban Presidential seal embroidered on the chest—drinking Cuban coffee, watching the sunrise over Big Bay.

"The honeymooners seemed to love it here," Danielle said.

"Did you hear that they were clocked by a sheriff's deputy going one hundred and ten?"

"No!"

"Yup, west of town on that straight stretch. He couldn't turn around fast enough to catch them, so he called Faith who read them the riot act that evening."

"I bet Marciana was driving."

"She was."

"Now it seems surreal that Fidel Castro stayed with us, slept in the bedroom right next to Chloe."

"She loves him. They spent every afternoon sitting in those chairs," Danielle said, pointing towards two wicker chairs pulled up to the railing, "looking down the valley and talking about stuff in Spanish."

They sipped the steaming coffee, looking at the red sky.

"Speaking of love, how'd Timothy take it when Dora told him she was leaving?"

"She told him on poker night. Timothy hugged her for a long time and said, 'I'm really happy for you. Love you, Dora.' By the way, Fidel is not a gracious loser. He accused Machete of cheating."

Danielle laughed. "He probably is. How did your conversation go with Ramona yesterday?"

"She asked me to consider becoming the assistant Director of Nursing. She's going to retire next spring. Wanted to know if you're coming back. I told her we'd talk it over."

"Do you really want to be saddled with all that administrative crap?"

"Not really."

"I think it would be exciting to buy a place in Marathon. We could work part-time. From there it's a short trip to Key West and Cuba, and we'll keep this place for our summer vacations," Danielle said, facing Stanley and standing very close.

"You do, huh? I'll call Karen at Fisherman's Hospital this afternoon and chat. I'm glad your daddy left us with his fortune."

Danielle laughed again. "Do you ever wonder what our lives would have been like if I'd have gone to Anchorage instead of Big Bay?"

"You'd have been married to a drug lord, weighing cocaine, and putting it in little baggies."

"I would not!"

She snuggled closer.

"We'd never have met Quinn and traveled to Cuba on the KEYWEST DREAMER. We'd never have met Fidel, Marco, and Marciana. I would never have met Timothy and The Usual Suspects. I would never have met the man I adore."

Stanley and Danielle embraced tightly, watching the tip of the sun peek up into the red sky over the peninsula.

"What's that old saying…red sky in the morning, sailors take warning?"

"Something like that," Stanley answered, squeezing Danielle tighter.

A green Volvo drove up the hill past the McMillen's condo. It turned around at the end of the block and returned. A lady wearing Brighton sunglasses studied the address number for several seconds.

...so here's where he lives...wonder if he'll recognize me...

Then she drove down the twisting road towards Big Bay. At the bottom of the hill she turned left, driving past the city park.

A young lady with long, blond hair sat on a park bench under a big sycamore tree. She lit a cigarette and turned her head, watching the Volvo drive past, the taillights eventually disappearing in the misty morning sunshine.

No Gray Twilights

Epilogue

"I hold it true, whate'er befall;
 I feel it, when I sorrow most;
'Tis better to have loved and lost
 Than never to have loved at all."

— *Alfred Tennyson*

To be continued…

Richard Alan Hall
lives in Traverse City, Michigan
with his wife, Debra Jean,
and their three dogs: Thelma, Hayden,
and a red-haired hussy named Lucy.
He writes in Traverse City, Michigan
and Key West, Florida.

In memory
of **Daisy**
who inspired
Little Miss

Original color photo by John Robert Williams Photography